Black Rain In Little Tokyo

A John Marlboro Novel

M. Ward Leon

黒い雨が降る リトル東京

ジョン・マールボロの小説

メートル・ウォード・レオン

Beacon Publishing Group
ISBN (Paperback): 978-1-961504-24-0

Black Rain In Little Tokyo
© 2025 M. Ward Leon

Cover Layout by Lori Pace
Edited by Gerard Hernandez

Beacon Publishing Group, New York, NY 10001
www.beaconpublishinggroup.com

Manufactured in the United States of America

For my Joanie & Meghan

Chapter One
The Yakuza

Black Rain is the Los Angeles chapter of the *yakuza*, also known as *gokudō*, "the extreme path," a transnational organized crime syndicate originating in Japan. They are known for their strict codes of conduct and several unconventional ritual practices, such as *yubitsume*, the Japanese ritual to atone for offenses or to show sincere apology and remorse to another by amputating the left little finger. This is because the sword cannot be held tightly in Japanese swordsmanship, and the little finger's grip is the tightest on the hilt. A little finger-amputee was, therefore, unable to grip his sword properly, weakening him in battle and making him more dependent on the protection of his boss.

Many have full-body tattoos known as *irezumi* and wear *fundoshi* (loincloth) with a kimono in private. When in public, they wear a Western-style suit covering them. Compared to the Cosa Nostra, the yakuza are regarded as the most sophisticated and wealthiest criminal organization.

The word yakuza is believed to have derived from a worthless hand in *Oicho-Kabu,* the Japanese card game similar to baccarat or blackjack.

When added up, the cards ya-ku-sa ("eight-nine-three") give the worst possible total. The origin of the yakuza themselves is difficult to determine. They are thought to have descended from gangs of rōnin who turned to banditry and defended villages from those same wayward samurai during the early 17th century. Their lineage may also be traced to bands of grifters and gamblers in Japan's feudal period.

Akio Watanabe lay bleeding in the alley behind the Hanashobu Hanaya, the flower shop that he and his family had owned for over ten years, his face looking like five pounds of ground Wagyu beef after the two gorillas dragged him out of his shop and beat him senseless for coming up short of the protection money that he owed to the Black Rain.

"Now, you owe another fifty dollars in addition to the hundred you already owe," The balled-headed thug called Yamato said.

Ichiro, the other leg-breaker, hissed, "Next time, I'll break both your kneecaps. We'll be back next week, and you better have the money. Understand?"

Akio said nothing as the two goons each gave another kick to his ribs.

"*Panku*! (punk)" Ichiro said, spitting down at Akio Watanabe as the bruisers walked away laughing.

It had been like this since the Los Angeles branch of the Yakuza moved into Little Tokyo two years ago. They quickly established an elaborate extortion, loan sharking, drugs, and money laundering organization. At first, many of the local merchants complained to the police. Those who dared to experience unexplained "accidents." Some fatal. The Japanese community soon fell in line and became mute.

Akio Watanabe gradually had the strength to pick himself up from the alley and went back inside his flower shop, where his wife, Keiko, was hiding. She screamed when she saw him, "Akio, *watashi no saiai* (my dearest), are you all right? Let me call Doctor Endo."

Akio stumbled to a wooden chair in the corner of the flower shop. He plopped down with a grunt. He shook his head, saying, "Keiko, *Ie* (no). I will be all right. It looks worse than it is."

"Akio. What are we to do?"

"We must pay."

"But where will he get the money?"

"I do not know. Maybe I will go seek the advice of the *shinshoku* (Shintō priest)." Aiko said.

The Shintō shrine sat behind the bright red torii gate on North San Pedro Street in Little Tokyo. Aiko walked under the torii, carefully looking around to see if he had been followed. As far as he could tell, he had not.

He walked under the Torii, then climbed the thirty-two stone stairs to the *sandō* (worshipper's path) that leads to the shrine. He stopped at the *chōzuya* (cleansing fountain) to rinse his face and hands in ritual purification before entering the *haiden* (hall of worship). Guarding the entrance were a pair of *komainu* statues. The statues are lion-like creatures meant to ward off evil spirits. They are carved of stone and usually are almost identical, but one has the mouth open, the other closed.

Before entering the temple, Aiko removed his shoes as a sign of reverence. He offered prayers to the *kami* (gods) there before speaking to the priest, *Bokushi* (Reverend) Haru Takahashi.

Bokushi Takahashi had been the spiritual leader of the Little Tokyo community since 1937, even during World War II, when all Japanese immigrants and Japanese Americans in the U.S. were sent to concentration camps. At that time, all Shintō shrines in the country were seized, and once the war was over, *Bokushi* Takahashi returned as head of the *Shintō Jinja Ritorutōkyō* (Shintō Shrine of Little Tokyo).

During the war, the Japanese community of Los Angeles was interred in the Manzanar Relocation Center located in the Owens Valley between the Sierra Nevada and the Inyo mountains; he was often the voice of reason and calm. The community saw *Bokushi* Takahashi as wise, sagacious, and perceptive beyond his eighty years.

Bokushi Takahashi spied Aiko deep in prayer, and when he felt it appropriate, he approached. As he got closer, he noticed that Aiko was injured. His face was swollen, and his eyes were blackened.

"Aiko san, what has happened to you?"

"*Sensei* (teacher), Keiko, and I are suffering much distress. Evil men are plaguing us, insisting that we pay them money. If we do not pay, they have threatened to burn our shop down and beat us."

"You must go to the police."

"Daiki Kaneko went to the police. Two weeks later, his body was found in a garbage can behind his restaurant, cut into several pieces." Aiko said.

"What did the police do?"

"Nothing. You know as well as I do that they do not concern themselves with what goes on in Little Tokyo."

"Do you know who these men are?" *Bokushi* Takahashi asked.

"They are members of the Yakuza. They are called the Black Rain, *Sensei*."

"Ah, yes. I have heard of them. Try not to worry. I will go to the police myself. Maybe they will listen to me."

"No, *Sensei*. You mustn't. They will come and attack you. They show no respect for anyone or anything!"

"Fear not, Aiko. I know someone on the police force."

Bokushi Takahashi arrived at LAPD Headquarters on 1st Street dressed in traditional vestments that drew many stares. He was wearing a *Jōsō*, the everyday garb of a Shintō priest. A loose red silk embordered robe hung past his knees, and under were purple silk billowing pants. He donned a tall purple hat called an *emboshi,* carried a baton called a *shaku* in his right hand, and wore low wooden clogs known as *asagutsu.*

Sergeant Dooley had been with the LAPD for over fifteen years. He thought that he had seen just about everything. As he was sitting at the front desk reading the sports section of the Los Angeles Times, he heard a commotion. The burly desk sergeant looked down from his perch high above the lobby floor, seeing the top of *Bokushi* Takahashi's head, and asked, "Can I help you?"

Before Takahashi could answer, some rookie cop shouted, "Hey, Sarge, isn't it a bit early for Halloween?"

Dooley answered, "Get your smart ass back out on patrol, or I'll have you pounding a beat in Watts, wise guy!"

"Sorry about that. What can I do for you, sir?" Dooley asked.

"I would like to see if Detective Sergeant Tanaka is available."

"And you are?"

"*Bokushi* Haru Takahashi."

"Yes, sir. Why don't you have a seat over there on the bench, and I'll check." Dooley said as he picked up the phone.

The detective picked up the phone on the third ring, "Tanaka."

"Detective, there is a *Bokushi* Haru Takahashi here to see you, sir," Dooley said.

"I'll be right there."

Tanaka gave a slight bow when he greeted the *Sensei.*

"*Bokushi* Takahashi, what can I do for you?"

"I must speak to you on a matter most urgent," The old man said.

"Please, come on back to my office."

Tanaka and the *Bokushi* made their way through the maze of hallways and offices to the Detective Squad room. The room was usually a buzz of activity and chatter, but as soon as they entered, it got eerily quiet. Everyone's attention was directed to the little Japanese man dressed in what they perceived to be a Halloween costume.

Detective Sergeant Tanaka barked, "Okay, people, this man is a Shintō priest, so just put your eyes back into your heads and show some respect!"

As if someone flipped a switch, the noise level went back up, and the commotion resumed the frantic pace that the squad room is known for.

Once inside Tanaka's office, he said, "*Bokushi* Takahashi, what can I do for you?"

"Villains are seizing our community, calling themselves Black Rain. They are said to be members of the ancient order of Yakuza."

"Yes. We are aware of them, *Sensei*. But until members of Little Tokyo are willing to come forth and testify against these thugs, there is little we can do," Tanaka said.

"Daiki Kaneko came to you for help, and the police did nothing, and he was killed. Is that not so?"

"I'm sorry to say that is true. It will take more than just one man but the whole Japanese community," Tanaka said.

"That will take some persuading. The people are scarcd."

"I understand. It might be best if I talk to the community. I will arrange a town hall meeting to discuss these issues and what people can do."

"I get the word out."

"Very good. In the meantime, I will see about beefing up the police presence and patrols in Little Tokyo."

"Thank you, Detective Tanaka."

"Do not despair, *Sensei*. I believe that things will get better, although it will take time and the courage of the community to overcome this threat."

"*Sayōnara*, Detective Tanaka."

"Goodbye, *Bokushi* Takahashi," Tanaka said.

The First Street North Community Center in Little Tokyo was filled to standing room only. There were over a hundred merchants there, all looking quite nervous. Detective Tanaka and *Bokushi* Takahashi sat with the Little Tokyo Community Council members on the podium. The room was buzzing with murmurs when Council President Botan Ito addressed the crowd. As Ito reached the lectern, he raised his hands to quiet the congregation; a hush came over the room.

"*Kon'nichiwa*," Ito said as he bowed to the audience.

There was a smattering of cordial greetings, but mostly, the crowd sat in silent anticipation, hopeful that a solution would end the plague that had descended upon their once peaceful community.

Ito smiled as he spoke, "Good people of Little Tokyo, we are gathered here tonight to see how we can best protect ourselves from these gangsters that have begun to prey upon us. That is why we've invited Detective Tanaka from the Los Angeles Police Department to come and speak with us this evening. Detective Tanaka."

Tanaka strolled to the podium, dressed in his police uniform rather than plain clothes. He felt it would give a better sense of authority and strength. There wasn't any applause or greetings from the crowd; Tanaka could feel tension, fear, and anger emanating from the assembly.

"*Kon'nichiwa.* I am Detective Sergeant Yuki Tanaka with the LAPD. I'm here tonight to talk to you about the infestation of the Black Rain in our community."

Someone from the back of the room shouted, "*Our* community?"

"That's right; I live not three blocks from here on East Second Street. I grew up and went to school here. My parents and I were rounded up and sent to Idaho to the Minidoka War Relocation Center in June 1942. So, yes, our community."

Dozens of people acknowledged and nodded, agreeing that they knew him and his family.

"Now, I know that many of you were afraid to attend this meeting, but let me stress that there is strength in numbers. I have already gotten approval from the department to have more police patrols and a more prominent police presence in Little Tokyo.

Don't think you can only count on your neighbors to do the work; it will take all of us. If you see something, you must say something. If you are harassed, you must report it. That is the only way we will drive these thugs out."

"That is easy for you, Detective. They aren't attacking you and beating your family," Doi Noguchi, the owner of the Lucky Dragon Restaurant, said.

"And you are?" Tanaka asked.

"I am Doi Noguchi, owner of the Lucky Dragon Restaurant."

"Have you been beaten, Mr. Noguchi?"

"I have. Also, my wife has been harassed, and my dumpster has been set on fire."

"Did you report any of this to the police?"

"They told me if I went to the police, they would kill my wife and me."

At this point, the audience grew angry, and Detective Sergeant Yuki Tanaka knew that the situation would get out of hand if he didn't take control.

Seated outside in an unmarked police van were two plainclothes Detectives, Jeffery Juneau and Charlie Bell. Detective Juneau was holding a Nikon Camera with a 200-millimeter lens filled with ultra-high-speed Kodak film specifically made to be used in low-level lighting situations and nighttime photography.

"Hey, Jeffery, here come a couple of gorillas. Be sure to get their photos. They look like trouble."

"Yeah, I see them. Let's get ready in case Tanaka might need us."

Inside the Community Center, the room became quiet once people realized the two Black Rain enforcers had entered.

Detective Tanaka spotted them as they made their way to the front of the room and, without saying a word, forced two people sitting in the front row to vacate their seats quickly.

"Ah, I see we have two latecomers. Gentlemen, may I have your names?"

"*Naze*?" Yamato sneered.

"Why? Because I like to get to know the people in our community."

"Do you know all of these people?" Yamato asked.

"As a matter of fact, I know most folks here."

"I am Yamato, and this is Itsuki. And who are you?"

"I'm Detective Sergeant Yuki Tanaka. I don't believe I've seen you two around before. Are you new to Little Tokyo?"

"Yesh. We are new to Little Tokyo. Is that a crime?"

"Not yet. What business are you in?" Tanaka asked.

"Oh, we're in high finance."

"Lending?"

"Collecting," Yamato wolfishly grinned and laughed.

As this back-and-forth was happening between Tanaka and the Yakuza thugs, people were leaving in droves; even the city council members snuck out. It looked like a stampede from a John Wayne Western. Once all the smoke had cleared, only Tanaka and *Bokushi* Takahashi were left on the dais.

When Detective Bell saw the people pouring out of the Center, he said, "Come on, Juneau, something's going down!"

When the detectives entered the hall, Detective Tanaka and the two Yakuza were the only ones there.

"Is everything all right, Sarge?" Bell asked.

"Yes, detectives, everything is fine. I was having a most enlightening conversation with these gentlemen."

Itsuki turned to see who Tanaka was speaking to. When he saw the two Caucasian officers, he uttered, "*Gaijin*." As if he was spitting.

Yamato didn't bother to turn around; he stood, as did his partner, and walked past Detectives Juneau and Bell without looking at them.

"What did he call us?" Juneau asked.

"*Gaijin*. It means foreigner. But it is also kind of an ethnic slur against non-Japanese people," Tanaka said, smiling.

"The cheeky bastards. So, what did you learn?" Bell asked.

"The people here are scared shitless. They aren't going to do anything. Any ideas?"

"I guess we can go undercover. Maybe have someone open a shop and see if the Black Rain preys upon them." Juneau said.

"If! Well, I can't do it, they've seen me. And they've seen you, too. We need to get an outsider. And I think I know just the guy." Tanaka said.

"Who?" Bell asked.

"A private dick. John Marlboro."

"Marlboro. He's a one-man wrecking crew. He leaves bodies lying around like peanut shells at a ball game." Juneau said.

"I heard about him. Didn't he put the whack on a dozen or so of Bugsy Siegel's henchmen?" Juneau asked.

"Yeah, that's the guy," Tanaka said.

Chapter Two
John Marlboro

The Moniker on the door read John Marlboro, Private Investigator, painted in gold letters on the door of his small one-room office in the Brockman Building, 700 South Grand Avenue, downtown Los Angeles.

The Brockman Building is a twelve-story Beaux-Arts building noted for its early use of multi-colored terra cotta and pioneering role in establishing West Seventh Street as downtown Los Angeles' premier shopping destination. Designed by Barnett, Haynes, and Barnett, the building features elaborate terra cotta detailing and a copper cornice – the only one in the city at the time of its construction in 1917.

Marlboro had a copy of Ring Magazine, the official rag of the boxing world, covering his face to help keep the sun's blinding rays from disturbing his sleep. His feet were up on the cluttered desk, littered with old, crumpled-up Los Angeles Times, an old beat-up, seldom-used Remington typewriter, and a chipped Libbey square ashtray that he procured from the Brown Derby Restaurant overflowing with the old Lucky Strike cigarette butts.

As he was beginning to drift off into a bit of REM sleep, he heard the handle of his office door jiggle. As he reached for his Colt – Official Police .38 Special- there came a thunderous knock on the door.

KNOCK! KNOCK!

"John! It's Detective Sergeant Yuki Tanaka. Open the door."

Marlboro shouted, "Hold your horses!"

He threw the magazine to the floor and strolled to the door. He unlocked it and rubbed the sleep out of his eyes while holding his pistol.

Tanaka looked down at the Colt and asked, "Expecting trouble?"

"When you've pissed off as many people as I have, you can't be too careful."

"I can see that. How would you like to piss off some more?"

"I'm listening. Come in and take a load off."

"How have you been?" Tanaka asked.

"I'm good. And you? It's been a long time."

"Yeah, too long. Sorry about that."

"Congratulations on making Sergeant," Marlboro said.

"Yeah, thanks. It took me long enough."

"Well, being partnered up with me probably didn't do your career any good."

"Probably not," Tanaka said, chuckling.

"Where do they have you working out of?"

"Little Tokyo."

"Why would they stick you there? Anyone with half a brain would put you in Little Italy," Marlboro said with a smirk.

"Really?"

"So, what can I do you for?"

"I have a job for you if you're interested."

"Dangerous?"

"Very," Tanaka said.

"Then I'm interested."

"You don't want to know what it's about?"

"Naw, I trust ya."

"Have you ever heard of the Yakuza?

"They're like the Japanese Mafia, aren't they?"

"That's right. They've begun operating in Little Tokyo. They are shaking down the Mom-and-Pop merchants for protection, loan sharking, selling drugs, and bringing in prostitution. They're calling themselves *Kuroi Ame*, Black Rain. I want you to pose as a merchant in Little Tokyo," Tanaka said.

"Why me, man?"

"I can't go. They've seen me and my two detectives. And you speak a little Japanese."

"Mostly just the curse words. *Gesu yarō*."

"Spoken like a true *Gaijin*," Tanaka said.

"But won't I stick out like a sore thumb? I honestly don't think I could pass for Japanese. Although I think I could do a better job than Marlon Brando did in the *Teahouse of the August Moon*."

"Not a problem. There are several non-Japanese shop owners in the neighborhood."

"But why not just use another policeman?"

"The brass doesn't want to."

"Why?" Marlboro pressed.

"They're afraid of the optics."

"Optics. What does that mean?"

"They're worried that the press will have a field day if this thing goes south."

"What exactly are they worried about?"

"A gangland-type war with the LAPD."

"So, what they're really looking for is a fall guy to pin it on if it turns out to be a clusterfuck. And since I ratted out some dirty cops a few years back, it's payback time for yours truly. Am I right?"

"That's how I read it, too. So, Whadda think?"

"What support can I expect?"

"Just what any normal citizen can expect."

"So that's none."

"Pretty much."

"What about weapons?"

"What about them?"

"I want to be able to use my entire arsenal. And I don't want any charges brought against me if I have to go in heavy!"

"Agreed."

"I want it in writing by Police Chief William H. Parker and Mayor Fletcher Bowron."

"Agreed. Anything else?" Tanaka asked.

"Yeah, my fee. I get twenty-five dollars a day plus expenses."

"Agreed."

"I assume the city is fronting the dough for the store. By the way, what type of store is it?" Marlboro asked.

"A paint store."

"Like artist's paints?"

"No. House paints."

"Am I doing this alone?"

"No. We've assigned an undercover police officer to help. Hana Wakabayashi."

"A woman?"

"Don't let the fact that she's a woman fool you. She rated top scores on the shooting range, plus she's a black belt in karate. She can kick your ass."

"Most women can," Marlboro quipped.

"I've asked her to meet me here."

"When?"

"Now," Tanaka answered.

KNOCK. KNOCK.

"Come in, Officer Wakabayashi," Tanaka said.

The door opened, and a five-foot-five vision of beauty walked in. Hana Wakabayashi was twenty-six, with raven black hair and alabaster skin worn in a bob cut. She was wearing her police uniform with a full complement duty belt.

"Officer Wakabayashi, this is John Marlboro. He's agreed to take on the assignment."

"Pleased to meet you, Mr. Marlboro. Detective Sergeant Tanaka has told me all about you," Wakabayashi said, holding out her hand.

"And you still want to work with me?" Marlboro said as he shook her hand.

She gave a quick look at Detective Tanaka, still seated.

"He's joking, Wakabayashi," Tanaka said, grinning.

"Have a seat, officer," Marlboro said as he gestured for her to sit beside Tanaka.

"Thank you."

"So, officer…"

"Hana, please," She said with a smile.

"So, Hana, are you okay with this assignment? Are you fully aware of the dangers involved? It's probably going to get ugly and messy."

"I'm prepared for the risks," She said.

"Officer Wakabayashi will pose as your wife; you will occupy the apartment above the paint store. While staging the paint shop, we will install extra safety locks, front and back, and bulletproof glass for the store and apartment windows. We'll also put in a heavy-duty fire sprinkler and fire alarm system. Oh, another precaution: a separate undercover phone with a direct line to the station and fire department," Tanaka explained.

"Sounds like you've thought of everything," Marlboro said.

"Any questions?" Tanaka asked.

"No, sir," Officer Wakabayashi said.

Tanaka looked at Marlboro, "Marlboro?"

"Back story?"

"We will complete it once you've accepted the assignment."

Marlboro smiled at Officer Wakabayashi and said, "I'm in if you are."

"I'm in," Wakabayashi said.

"Good. I'll get back to you both once the story is complete. It should take a couple of days. In the meantime, I suggest you two grab some lunch and get to know each other," Tanaka suggested.

As Tanaka approached the door, Marlboro said, "Don't forget about the signed agreement."

"I'll have it messengered to you by the end of day."

Once he was gone, Marlboro said, "How about grabbing a bite to eat?"

"Sounds good. Where?"

"Ever been to The Original Pantry Café?"

"No."

"You'll love it. I go there just about every day."

As they sat down, Marlboro asked, "So, Hana, what do you think of The Original Pantry Café?"

"Interesting," she said, trying to be polite. But what she really thought was, 'What a dump.'

Betty, the waitress, came over with two plastic-covered menus. She handed them each one and asked, "Hey, Johnny boy, what can I get you to drink?"

"Hey, doll. I'll have a Bull Dog Stout. And the lady will have?"

"Oh, I'll just have a Coke."

"One brewski and an Atlanta special coming up," Betty said with a smile.

Looking around at all the characters in the café, Hana smiled and said, "So, you come here every day?"

"Yeah, I know it's not the Polo Lounge, but the food's good, it's cheap, and there are more characters here than in Central Casting. And what a private dick pockets after all the expenses; good and cheap ain't bad, doll."

"Sorry, I didn't mean anything by it."

"It's Jake, doll."

After Betty set the drinks on the table, she asked, "Have you decided?"

Marlboro looked at Hana to see if she had made a decision.

"I think I'll have a hamburger. Well done," Hana said.

"Johnny?" Betty asked.

"I'll do the burger, rare, and a side of French fries."

On the way back to the kitchen, Betty shouted, "One Hockey Puck, One on the hoof, and make it cry with a side of Joan of Arc."

Once the waitress had left, Marlboro asked his soon-to-be partner, "So, Hana, what are your thoughts on taking on the Black Rain? Scared?"

"A little. You?"

"I'd be a fool not to be. But I've dealt with mobsters before."

"Yeah, I heard you had a bit of a run-in with Bugsy Siegel and his gang. How many bodies did you rack up?"

"I don't keep count. I leave that to the fish wrappers."

"But don't the newspapers always inflate the numbers?"

"That's Jake with me; so much the better," Marlboro said with a devilish grin.

Betty, the waitress, came and placed their meals in front of them. "Will there be anything else?"

"We're good for now, doll," Marlboro said.

"Enjoy," Betty said.

"Have you ever had to use your weapon, Officer Wakabayashi?" Marlboro asked.

"Why do you ask?"

"Well, there's a good chance that you'll have to use it on this assignment, and I need to know that you won't hesitate if we get into a jam."

"No. I haven't had to use my weapon. But I assure you that I won't hesitate to use it if the time comes."

"*When* the time comes."

"When the time comes," Wakabayashi said.

Marlboro stared at Hana, looking to see if she showed any sign of flinching. Satisfied, he said, "Okay. Let's eat."

After a few minutes, he asked, "How's the burger?"

"Good, but next time, we're going for sushi."

After lunch, Marlboro returned to his office as Wakabayashi went back on duty. While waiting to hear back from Detective Sergeant Tanaka, he opened his gun safe and cleaned all his weaponry, ensuring they were all in working order. He then inventoried his ammunition and compiled a list of which weapons needed more ammo.

A knock came on Marlboro's office door a little before five o'clock. His desk was littered with no less than twelve guns, including such weapons as a 9mm Parabellum Browning machine pistol, .45 Colt automatic pistol, Ithaca Model 1911 A1 .45 pistol, Colt – Official Police .38 Special, .32 caliber Colt Detective Special 'snub-nosed' revolver, Semi-automatic Colt M1911 .45 caliber, Walther PPK pistol, Browning A5 12-gauge shotgun, even a Thompson submachine gun, or "Tommy Gun," *aka* "the Chicago typewriter, and a military-grade Browning Automatic Rifle BAR.

"Come in!" Marlboro shouted.

Detective Sergeant Tanaka opened the door and stopped in his tracks; his jaw dropped as he saw what lay on Marlboro's desk.

"My God, Marlboro. I haven't seen this much firepower since we landed at Omaha Beach."

"I'm not taking any chances with these *kamikaze* motherfuckers. So, what brings you down here?"

"I have the signed agreement signed by Police Chief William H. Parker and Mayor Fletcher Bowron," Tanaka said.

"I thought you were going to have it messengered over."

"Well, I wanted to hear your thoughts about Officer Wakabayashi."

"She looks good on paper. You do know we're in for a tough slog. I just hope we both come out of this in one piece. Because once we tell the Black Rain to go fuck themselves, all Hell is going to break out."

"That's what I figure, too. That's why I brought you this," Tanaka said as he passed Marlboro a cardboard box.

"Hey, brother, it's not my birthday."

Marlboro opened the box and found a bulletproof vest inside. He held it up in front of him and said, "I've heard about these things. Do they really work?"

"Oh yeah. They can stop most handgun rounds," Tanaka said.

"Most?"

"It's saved a dozen cops on the force this year alone. Hopefully, they won't break out the heavy artillery."

"If they do this thing, ain't going to do much good. Hey, *Arigatō*."

"*Dōitashimashite*. Wear it in good health." Tanaka said as he headed towards the door.

"*Sayōnara*, Tanaka-san."

"*Sayōnara*, Marlboro-san."

Chapter Three
The Back Story

While he waited to get the back story from Detective Tanaka and the brass downtown, Marlboro decided to drive by the paint shop and do a bit of surveillance of the area. He drove his fire-engine red 1946 Chevrolet Fleetmaster Convertible twice around the block. The paint store was sandwiched between the Mikado and Little Tokyo hotels. Both hotels are considered historic landmarks; both have been around since the early 1900s.

Marlboro noted that the name of the paint shop was going to be *Natsukashī Kokoro*, Nostalgic Heart. It sounds pleasant enough until the shooting stars. He parked across the street and began taking photographs of the paint store and the entire area. He got out of his car and acted as a tourist, taking pictures all up and down East First Street. He strolled down the alley, taking photographs to see what peril they could be in when the shit hits the fan.

Once he had completed his mission, he carefully observed if he was being followed. He discovered that he was being tailed. He figured he was considered suspicious because he was a *Gaijin* taking too much interest in Little Tokyo. Losing the tail took only two miles since he was an expert in ducking tails. When he shot down into his office parking garage, he was free and clear of the black Lincoln that had desperately tried to stay with him.

After he parked the Fleetmaster deep down on the third-floor level, he waited to ensure he had lost his tail.

Marlboro switched sports coats to change his appearance, just in case. He had learned the hard way not to be too lax when dealing with professionals. He then took the stairs up three flights to the street. All clear.

He took the elevator up to his office. Once inside, he locked the door and placed the .45 Colt automatic pistol he had tucked behind his back on the desk. He sat down and called Detective Sergeant Tanaka.

"Detective Sergeant Tanaka."

"Yuki, Marlboro here."

"Hey, John, what's up?"

"I wanted to let you know I just got back from scoping out the paint store."

"Thoughts?"

"It's got pros and cons. The biggest con is that it sits between the Mikado and Little Tokyo hotels."

"Yeah, I know, but it was our only viable option."

"That's what I figured. But that may also turn out to be a good thing. I don't think the Black Rain will want to be responsible for destroying two city landmarks. That would bring a shitstorm down upon their heads from the city, especially if a bunch of civilians got caught in the crossfire," Marlboro said.

"John, just try and make sure it's not you who gets them in your crossfire."

"That's not my style. You know that, Yuki."

"I know," Tanaka said.

"When is the store estimated to open?" Marlboro asked.

"If all goes according to plan, next week. I'll have your back story ready for you tomorrow afternoon."

"I like the store's name. Did you think it up?"

"No, Officer Wakabayashi came up with Nostalgic Heart. *Natsukashī Kokoro*, you like it? I'm a bit surprised; it's not very macho."

"Aw, Yuki, you know I'm just a big softy."

"Yeah, right. A big softy with a body count larger than Douglas MacArthur's Army."

"MacArthur was a pussy," Marlboro said, laughing.

Tanaka let that comment slide and said, "I'll call you tomorrow when I get the back story ready for you."

"Okay, I look forward to hearing from you. Maybe we can do lunch."

CLICK.

Marlboro deliberately omitted the part about his being followed—no need to get Tanaka all bent out of shape at this point. There will be plenty of sleepless nights in store for Detective Sergeant Tanaka, the LAPD, and Little Tokyo.

At this point, Detective Sergeant Tanaka, the LAPD, and Little Tokyo will have plenty of sleepless nights in store.

Marlboro arranged to meet Tanaka at his old stomping grounds, The Original Pantry Café, for lunch at one o'clock. Even though the café was within walking distance, Marlboro liked driving his red Fleetmaster, but he decided to walk just in case the Black Rain was still looking for him.

Detective Sergeant Tanaka was waiting for him outside when he arrived.

"Been waiting long?" Marlboro asked.

"About ten minutes. Why are you walking? Something happened to your car?"

"No. Just felt like walking. It's such a nice day."

Tanaka grinned and said, "Marlboro, come on, man. Nobody walks in L.A., even six blocks, unless there's something wrong with their car. So, tell me what's going on,"

"Okay, but let's go inside and grab a table. If we stand out here and yak, we'll be sitting at the counter," Marlboro said as he led the way into the restaurant.

Joanie, the head waitress, greeted them as they walked in. "Hey Johnny boy, what's the story, morning glory?"

"Not much, doll. Same old, same old."

"Come on; I've saved your booth for you."

Tanaka jabbed Marlboro in the ribs, "I am impressed, your own booth. Swanky."

"Shut up," Marlboro said.

"Here you go. I'll bring you, boys, a couple of menus," Joanie said as she seated them.

Once seated, Tanaka asked, "All right, Marlboro, why are you really walking?"

"Okay, I didn't want to mention it. Yesterday, when I was doing recon on the store, I guess a couple of Black Rain members must have become suspicious of me and tried to tail me."

"Oh, great!"

"But I lost them before I got to my office."

"Are you sure?"

"Positive. However, my fire-engine red Fleetmaster stands out like a sore thumb. So, I would ask if you can issue Officer Wakabayashi an unmarked and untraceable car and me."

"I think that's a good idea. I'll make sure we get you something boring, drab, and dull," Tanaka said with a grin.

The waitress, Joanie, brought the menus, "Can I get you boys something to drink? Johnny, the usual?"

"Yeah, doll, I'll have a Bull Dog Stout," Marlboro replied.

"And for you, dreamboat?"

"I'll have what he's having," Tanaka said.

"Right, two oat sodas, coming right up. I'll be back for your order when I bring the brewskis," She said as she trotted off to get the beers.

Minutes later, Joanie brought two bottles of Bull Dog Stout.

"What can I get you, boys?" She asked.

"Yuki, what looks good to you?" Marlboro asked.

"How's the beef stew?"

"Great," Marlboro said.

"I'll try the beef stew," Tanaka said.

"And for you, as if I don't know," Joanie said, grinning at Marlboro.

"The usual, Joanie."

"Shocking," Joanie said as she headed towards the cook's station.

"Cookie, I got one Bossy in a bowl and one on the hoof, and make it cry with a side of Joan of Arc," she shouted to the cook.

"Got it. And tell Marlboro, Cookie says, Hey." The crusty old chef said, not bothering to look up from his food prep.

While they waited for their lunch, Marlboro thought he'd ask about the mission's back story.

"So, tell me about my new life, or should I say my old life," He said.

As Tanaka handed Marlboro a manila envelope, he said, "It's all in here."

"Well, how about you just give me the skinny, so's I don't have to burn my peepers over lunch?"

"Your name is Butch Baker; you were a pilot during the war. You flew B-25s in the Pacific. After the war, you were stationed in Yokohama for three years, where you met Aiko. Her parents were killed in the bombing of Hiroshima.

You met her in a sushi bar where she worked as a waitress. You dated for the last two years of your service in Japan. You were married in Tokyo in a civil service. Once you got shipped back to the States, you sent for Aiko. You're originally from Van Nuys, an only child, and your parents are deceased. You decided to live in Little Tokyo to give Aiko a sense of community since she is leaving her homeland and culture."

"I'm sure one heck of a swell guy," Marlboro quipped.

"Yeah, you're a real pip," Tanaka said.

"Why a paint store?" Marlboro asked.

"You worked in a paint store in Van Nuys before the war. So, you decided to use the G.I. Bill to open your own place. It's all in here, so read it and memorize it. I've given one to Hana, too."

Marlboro folded the envelope into his coat pocket just as Joanie brought their lunch.

"One Bossy in a bowl for you and one burger, rare with 'O' and a side of fries. Can I get you, boys, anything else? How 'bout it, dreamboat?" She said, flirting with Tanaka.

Tanaka smiled and said, "I could use some crackers."

She reached inside her apron, plopped a couple of packets of saltines on the table, and said, "A couple of dog biscuits for the copper."

"How do you know I'm a copper?" Tanaka asked.

"Marlboro only brings dames or coppers here. And since you ain't a doll, you must be a copper."

"Guilty as charged," Tanaka said.

"You hitched, copper?"

"No."

She took out her order pad, scribbled her phone number, tore off the page, and handed it to Tanaka. "Here, cute stuff, call me sometime. And lunch is on me."

Tanaka looked at the page and smiled, "Thanks, Joanie."

"Hey, Doll, how about me? Is my lunch free, too?"

"No," She said as she walked away giggling.

Marlboro looked at Tanaka sitting there with a big grin on his face.

"Wipe that smirk off your face, dreamboat."

Officer Hana Wakabayashi took it upon herself to do precisely what Marlboro did. She went to Little Tokyo to do a bit of recon. Unlike her soon-to-be fake husband, she went unnoticed. She went all around and talked to many shop owners, not about the Black Rain, but just about introducing herself and making some connections. Afterward, she went to Marlboro's office.

KNOCK. KNOCK.

Marlboro opened the top drawer in his desk, slid his hand in, and grabbed hold of the Colt–Police .38 Special. Then called out, "Come in. It's open."

Wakabayashi swung the door open and said, "Honey, I'm home."

"*Kon'nichiwa*, Aiko-*chan*, I've missed you."

Hana closed the door, plunked down in a chair opposite Marlboro, and kicked her feet onto the corner of the desk. She sat there with a big grin, her arms crossed behind her head.

"Why so smug?" Marlboro asked as he eased his finger off the trigger of the .38 Special.

"Well, I went to Little Tokyo and checked out *Natsukashī Kokoro*."

"Did you now."

"Yes, I did. I also took a bunch of snapshots. I just got them back from Walgreens. Here, take a look," She said as she tossed the brown and green envelope onto the desk.

He opened the top drawer of his desk and tossed a similar Walgreens brown and green envelope at her.

"Here, I took these yesterday," He said.

Wakabayashi and Marlboro thumbed through each other's photos. When they were finished, Marlboro asked, "Did you draw any interest from anybody?"

"No. Did you?"

"As a matter of fact, I did. I picked up a tail on my way back to my office. But I managed to lose them."

"Did you happen to see who they were?"

"No. I just know it was a couple of goons in a black Lincoln."

"Did you tell Detective Tanaka?"

"No."

"Why not?" She asked.

"I didn't want to put the kibosh on the deal."

"Do you think he'd do that?"

"No, not him. But who knows what the brass might do. So, just keep it under your hat. I did ask Tanaka for a less conspicuous car when we finally open the store."

"Why do you think they followed you?"

"I guess they thought that I looked suspicious. A white guy going around taking photographs that didn't seem kosher."

"Why didn't they think you were just a tourist?"

"As you can see, I was taking a lot of photos of the alley and other non-touristy things, " he said, gesturing to his photographs.

"I guess it raised suspicions."

"Yeah, I guess so. I wouldn't have thought these tough guys would be so touchy."

"Probably a prelude of things to come."

"It's not too late for you to back out if you're having second thoughts," Marlboro said.

"No way."

"Good. I'm glad, Mrs. Baker."

"Me too, Mr. Baker."

Marlboro said, "Just call me Butch."

Chapter Four
Yubitsume

The paint store was ready to open at the beginning of the following week. Marlboro and Hana drove to the store to give the place the once over and have furniture moved into their apartment above the store. The store was well stocked with Sherwin-Williams Paints and accessories. The Sherwin-Williams Paints representative was there to give them a crash course in what it takes to be a Sherwin-Williams Paint franchisee.

"Mr. Baker, Mrs. Baker, I'm George Bell, your Sherwin-Williams Paints representative. I'm here to answer any questions you might have concerning the operation of your Sherwin-Williams Paint franchise."

"It's a pleasure to meet you, Mr. Bell. My wife, Aiko, and I have been reviewing the franchise and marketing materials your company provided us. And at the moment, I think we're pretty much up to speed."

"That's great. I just thought I would stop by and introduce myself and let you know that you can contact me anytime if you have any questions that may come up. Here's my card with my office number. Please get in touch with me with any concerns; we at Sherwin-Williams Paints want you to succeed and will do anything we can to see that you are."

"That's very kind of you," Hana said.

"Well, it was a pleasure meeting you both. And good luck," Bell said as he left the store.

Moments later, while Marlboro and Hana were in the back room, they heard the bell above the front door ring.

"I'll go see who that is," Marlboro said.

Standing at the entrance stood two rather large Japanese men dressed in ill-fitting suits, looking rather ominous.

"I'm sorry, but we're not open yet. We don't open until next week," Marlboro explained.

"Mr. Baker?" Yamato inquired.

"That's right. And you are?"

"A friend."

"You don't look like any friend that I know."

"I am your new friend."

"Oh, I see. And what's your name, new friend?"

"Yamato."

"Yamato. And is this another new friend?"

"That's right. His name is Itsuki."

"No last names, just Yamato and Itsuki?"

"That's right."

"Well, Yamato and Itsuki, don't take this the wrong way, but I already have enough friends for now. But I'll let you know as soon as I need to add to my friend list." Marlboro said with a smile.

"You don't understand. We're not asking. We're telling," Itsuki said.

"Oh, he does speak. I was beginning to wonder."

"A wise guy. Making with the funny stuff," Yamato said.

Hana appeared from the back room, "Honey, who are these gentlemen?"

"Well, this fella here is Yamato, and the other is Itsuki. No last names. They've stopped by to let us know that they want to be our new best friends. They're very insistent," Marlboro said with a wink and smile.

"That's very nice of you boys to stop by. But we're busy getting ready to open our store next week. So, why don't you come back when we open."

Yamato slid his jacket open to reveal a pistol stuck in the waistband of his pants. "Look, honey, Mr. Yamato has a pistol," Hana said innocently.

"Why, so he does. May I see it?" Marlboro asked.

Yamato pulled the .45 Colt automatic pistol out and pointed it at Marlboro to intimidate him. Marlboro took a step forward and, in a wink of an eye, snatched the pistol out of the big man's hand and pointed it at him and his partner.

Hana sweetly said, "That is one very nice pistol, Mr. Yamato. But you really shouldn't be pointing a gun at someone. That's very rude and careless."

Marlboro pointed the pistol at Itsuki and asked, "Do you have a gun as well, Mr. Itsuki?"

Itsuki nodded.

"May I see it?" Hana asked.

Itsuki slowly removed his pistol and carefully handed it to Hana.

"Ooh, this is a nice one too. You know what? I think we'll just keep these here in our safe until the opening day of our paint store. Then you boys can come by and collect them. How does that sound?" Hana asked.

Yamato and Itsuki stood looking at each other dumbfounded.

"Now, you fellas, be sure to stop by next week for the grand opening. We look forward to seeing you, and be sure to tell your friends to stop by if they need any paint. But for now, hit the bricks. Scram," Marlboro said.

"What do you mean they took your guns!" Shouted Black Rain's overlord, Kio Kobayashi.

Kobayashi sat crossed-legged on a *tatami* mat at the head of a long mahogany *chabudai* (short-legged table) with his lieutenants, Aoi Yamaguchi, Minato Aoki, and Kenji Yamamoto, flanked on either side of the table, with Yamato and Itsuki seated at the far end of the table opposite Kobayashi. In front of them was a folded piece of beautifully woven *kasuri* cotton cloth.

Standing on Kobayashi's right side was Ichiro, his *kyaputen* (captain). He was dressed in the traditional samurai dress, a *kamishimo*, a two-piece garment worn over a silk kimono. Ichiro carried three traditional samurai swords: the longest, the Tachi, the Katana, and the Wakizashi. He stood motionless, always at the ready with his hand on the Tachi.

"You two idiots are worthless!" The *oyabun* (boss) screamed.

Kobayashi removed two *tantōs* (short swords) underneath the table and slid them towards Yamato and Itsuki over the highly polished tabletop. They each took the sword in their right hand, unsheathed the *tantō*, and placed the weapon carefully in front of them.

Kobayashi stared at the henchmen and forcefully uttered, "*Yubitsume*! (the cutting off a portion of one's left little finger above the top knuckle)."

Yamato and Itsuki each knew what was expected of them. It was the price they were to pay for bringing shame upon their *oyabun*.

They bowed, then placed their left hand face down on the small *kasuri* cloth. Picking up the *tantō*, they slowly cut off a portion of their left little finger above the top knuckle of the finger. The crackling and crunching of the distal phalanges as the sword's blade cut through the bone.

After tying off the bleeding stump, they wrapped the severed portion of their finger in the *kasuri* cloth and graciously and apologetically submitted the "package" to Kobayashi, their *oyabun* (boss).

"*Owabi moushi agemasu, oyabun* (I apologize, boss)." Yamato and Itsuki said in unison as they bowed their heads, touching the tabletop.

Kobayashi took the "packages," placed them to his left, and without any sign of gratitude, said, "Go."

Yamato and Itsuki left the Yakuza headquarters and walked the six blocks to the Japanese Hospital, where they knew they would receive medical attention without police interference.

"May I help you?" The nurse at the front desk asked.

Yamato and Itsuki held up their bleeding hands. Yamato said, "We need to see a doctor."

Unfazed, the seasoned nurse picked up the hospital phone and said, "Have a seat over there. And I'll get someone to see you."

Nurse Aikawa, sixty-two, had been a nurse for over forty years. She had seen dozens of these Yakuza goons come into the hospital with these self-inflicted injuries. Some had come in so often that they had just a couple of fingers left. Those were the major fuck-ups of the organization, who were only asked to carry out the simplest of tasks. One look at these two, and she knew she was looking at repeat customers.

The phone rang, and Nurse Aikawa answered it; she listened, nodded, and addressed the two hooligans, "You can go on back. The second room on the left."

Yamato and Itsuki walked back to the patient's room, dripping blood.

A voice was heard over the hospital intercom, asking, *"Will maintenance please come to the lobby? Clean up is requested."*

While Yamato and Itsuki waited to see a doctor, a young nurse entered the room holding two clipboards to gather their information. She was surprised to see both men holding up their left hands with what appeared to her to be the same injury.

"Can you fill out these forms, or shall I assist you?" She asked.

"We can fill them out," Itsuki said.

"How long before we can see the doctor?" Yamato asked with a wince.

The nurse handed each a clipboard and said, "As soon as you complete these forms, the doctor will see you."

She took their blood pressure and temperature as they filled out the forms.

Once they had completed the forms, which most of the information was false, they then handed the clipboards back to the young nurse, who gave the forms a quick glance and asked, "So, Mr. Smith and Mr. Jonze, I need to ask you how do you gentlemen intend on paying for your visit?"

Yamato reached into his blood-soaked pants pocket, pulled out a wad of twenty-dollar bills, and said, "Take what you need doll."

She peeled off one hundred dollars and left the room. On her way out, she said, "The doctor will be in shortly, " closing the door behind her.

Moments later, there was a faint knock on the door, and before either could answer, a man in a white lab coat entered the room wearing a stethoscope around his neck.

The name tag on his lab coat read, "Doctor Yamaguchi."

He looked at them and said, unfazed, "I'm Doctor Yamaguchi. Ah, *Yubitsume*. Okay, who wants to go first?"

Yamato said, "I'll go first."

"Come over here by the sink," Yamaguchi ordered.

The nurse came in with bandages, scissors, and surgical tape.

After Doctor Yamaguchi washed and bandaged the wound, he had Yamato sit with his hand elevated above his heart. He then did the same procedure to Itsuki.

"Now you both sit tight and don't move. I'll be back in ten minutes to check on you. Nurse Machida will be here with you to make sure either of you show any signs of shock."

Once the doctor left, Yamato gestured that he and Itsuki should go.

"You're not going anywhere until the Doctor says so," Nurse Machida said sternly as she leaned against the door defiantly.

When Yamaguchi returned, he gave Yamato and Itsuki a quick exam and proclaimed they were fit to leave.

"Come back in a week to have your bandages changed unless you experience redness, swelling, fever, pus, or a bad smell. If you notice any of these symptoms, get in here immediately. Understand?" Yamaguchi asked.

"*Hai*," Yamato said.

Yamaguchi waited for Itsuki's response; when he did not, he said, "Understand?"

Reluctantly, Itsuki answered, "*Hai*."

"Okay, you both can go," Doctor Yamaguchi said.

Yamato decided that they needed to save face with the *oyabun*. So, his plan was for him and Itsuki to return to the paint store and kick the living shit out of the *gaijin* and his *baishunpu* (whore) to show Kobayashi that they had redeemed themselves.

"Do you think that this is a good idea? Not informing *oyabun*. It could get us in deeper shit," Itsuki said.

"*Oyabun* wants warriors, not *koshinukes* (cowards)!"

"Okay, so, what's your plan?" Itsuki asked.

"We'll wait until we're feeling better in a day or two, and then when they have their opening, we'll hang around until they're ready to close, and then we'll strike."

"Kill them?"

"No! We will teach them a lesson they'll never forget," Yamato said with a wolfish grin.

Detective Tanaka stopped by the *Natsukashī Kokoro* paint store dressed in plain clothes to check on Marlboro and Officer Wakabayashi's progress.

"So, Marlboro, how goes it?" Tanaka asked.

"Good. Everything is going along as planned."

"I'm glad to hear it. Officer Wakabayashi, how are you doing? Are you blending into the community?"

"Oh, yes, sir. We've already made contact with the Black Rain."

"Oh?"

"After the Sherwin-Williams Paint representative stopped by, two Yakuza thugs came into the store and threatened us with pistols," Wakabayashi said.

"Uh-huh. And then what happened?" Tanaka asked in a tone that he sensed he already knew the answer.

"Well, when one of them pulled his weapon, Marlboro snatched the pistol away from the man and disarmed the other of his gun. Sending them off packing, sir," Wakabayashi explained.

"I see. That might explain the call I got from the Japanese Hospital yesterday about two men being treated for *yubitsume*," Tanaka said.

"What's that?" Marlboro asked.

"It's a Japanese ritual to atone for offenses to show sincere apology to their overlord by amputating a portion of their little finger," Tanaka said.

"You got to have a real pair of balls to whack off a bit of your finger. I don't know too many gunsels that would have the guts to do that," Marlboro said.

"You need to be careful. I'm sure these guys will be wanting to exact their revenge on you two. Do not hesitate to call in the Marines if you get the slightest sense of getting into a jam. Understood?"

"Yes, sir," Wakabayashi said.

"Marlboro?"

"Oh, I think that we'll be able to handle a couple of schizoid finger-whacking spazzes."

Opening day for *Natsukashī Kokoro* brought many of the community's fellow shop owners to welcome the Bakers.

All members of the Little Tokyo City Council were present. Council President Botan Ito, Hideo Adachi, Kaede Bushida, Haoki Endo, Naoki Hara, and Touma Kubo are all store owners.

Akio Watanabe and his wife Keiko, the owners of *Hanaya Mise* (florist shop), stopped by not only to welcome the Bakers but also to warn them about the dangers of going against the Black Rain. Akio was still showing the signs of the beating that he had endured.

He pulled Marlboro aside, leaving his wife, Keiko, to talk to Wakabayashi.

"You must be careful," Warned Akio. "I missed one protection payment, and they beat me senseless. They threatened not only my wife, Keiko, but also my children. Mr. Baker, these men will not think twice about inflicting harm upon you and Mrs. Baker."

"Thank you, Akio-san. I appreciate your telling me. I will take heed. And please, it's Butch and Aiko," Marlboro said with a slight bow.

Council President Botan Ito walked up to Marlboro and Watanabe and asked, "Watanabe-san, how are you feeling?"

"I am on the mend, President Botan-san." Watanabe said.

"I am glad to hear it. Might I have a word with Mr. Baker alone?" Botan said.

"Yes, of course. It was very nice meeting you, Butch. Please come by my flower shop anytime; I would love to show you around. *Sayōnara*."

"*Sayōnara*, Watanabe-san." Marlboro said.

Botan waited until Watanabe was out of earshot before speaking.

"Mr. Baker."

"Butch, please," Marlboro said.

"Butch. I want you to be aware that we have a slight problem with some Japanese mobsters called the Black Rain. They have been extorting our citizens, and when they don't or can't pay, they attack them physically, like Mr. Watanabe."

"What about the police?" Marlboro asked.

"We've asked the police for their help, and they have increased police patrols and even put more police on the beat. But as soon as the police leave, they swoop in."

"What is the City Council encouraging the shop owners to do? Comply or resist?"

"It would be nice if we could band together and fight back, but I'm afraid most people just knuckle under. They are scared. You must do what your conscience dictates if they approach you, Butch."

"Botan-san, thank you for the heads up. Aiko and I will be vigilant."

Marlboro noticed Yamato and Itsuki loitering across the street as the gathering was winding down, looking suspicious. He whispered to Wakabayashi, "I see our friends across the street, so be prepared. I'm going to get us a couple of pistols."

He went into the back of the store and got Wakabayashi a .32-caliber Colt Detective Special 'snub-nosed' revolver and a .45-caliber Colt automatic pistol for himself.

Yamato and Itsuki entered when some people were still in the shop. Yamato announced, "Okay, the store is now closed. Get out!"

The remaining people scrambled out the door.

"Oh, look, honey, what the cat dragged in. What do you jamokes want?" Marlboro asked.

Wakabayashi was standing close to Yamato when he pulled out his gun. Before Itsuki could get his gun out, Wakabayashi gave a karate kick to Yamato's wrist, sending his Walther PPK pistol high into the air. While Yamato and Itsuki watched the gun sail away, Marlboro pulled his Colt out and said, "Okay, you mugs, get your hands up, or I'll drill ya!"

As Wakabayashi disarmed Itsuki of his weapon, she said, "Both of you, get down on your knees with your hands behind your heads."

"This ought to put you in solid with your boss," Marlboro said.

Wakabayashi asked, "Should we call the cops?"

"Nay, I think them having to chop off another knuckle will be a worse punishment than sitting in a cell downtown. Don't you?"

"Oh, yeah," Wakabayashi said.

"But before we let you goombahs go. I'd like to know who your boss is." Marlboro said, poking Yamato in the head with his Colt.

"*Shinjimae*!" Yamato grunted.

"What did he say?" Marlboro asked Wakabayashi.

He said, "Go to Hell."

"That wasn't very nice," Marlboro said as he grabbed Yamato's finger stump and squeezed.

"*AAIEEEEEHHHH*!" Yamato screamed as tears of pain rolled down his face.

"I'll ask you again. Who's your boss?"

"*Fakkuyū* (fuck you)!" Yamato winched.

Marlboro looked at Wakabayashi for translation.

She said, "Fuck you."

Marlboro squeezed Yamato's finger stump again and, this time, twisted it, causing it to start bleeding profusely.

"*AAIEEEEEHHHH*!" Yamato screamed at the top of his lungs as he fell to the floor unconscious.

Marlboro moved behind Itsuki, took hold of his finger, and asked, "Who's your boss?"

Itsuki didn't hesitate, "Kio Kobayashi."

"Who are the lieutenants?"

"Aoi Yamaguchi, Minato Aoki, Kenji Yamamoto."

"Just so you don't look like you squealed," Marlboro said as he twisted Itsuki's finger until it too bled.

"*AAIEEEEEHHHH*!"

"Now, take your goombah and get out. If I ever see either of you in this shop again, I'll kill you both, understand?"

"*Hai*," Itsuki said.

Yamato and Itsuki wobbled their way out of the shop, sobbing.

Marlboro locked the door, turned to Wakabayashi, and said, "Well, I thought that went rather well. Don't you?"

Chapter Five
Yubitsume Part 2

"They took your guns again!" Screamed *oyabun* Kio Kobayashi.

Kobayashi was again seated cross-legged at the head of the *chabudai*, flanked on either side by his lieutenants. Yamato and Itsuki were sitting at the far end of the table opposite Kobayashi. Once again, the woven *kasuri* cotton cloth was placed before them.

"Did I tell you to go back to *Natsukashī Kokoro*!" Kobayashi barked.

"*Īe* (no)," Yamato answered, his head bowed, touching the tabletop.

"So, why did you?"

"We wanted to gain favor with you, *oyabun*."

"And because of your incompetence, you brought disgrace and shame to yourselves, me, and the Black Rain!"

"*Shazai itashimasu, Dono* (my deepest apology, master)."

Once again, Kobayashi removed two *tantōs* (short swords) underneath the table and slid them towards Yamato and Itsuki. They each took the sword in their right hand, unsheathed the *tantō*, and placed the weapon carefully in front of them.

"*Yubitsume!*" Kobayashi growled.

They bowed, then placed their left hand face down on the small *kasuri* cloth. Trying not to show fear, they Picked up the *tantō*, unwrapped the bandages, and slowly cut off another portion of their left little finger. The pain was ten times worse than the first time, but they both gritted their teeth and endured the excruciating agony.

Afterward, they tied off the bleeding stump, wrapped the severed portion of their finger in the *kasuri* cloth, and submitted the "package" to Kobayashi.

Before they could speak, Kobayashi raised his hand to silence them. He then took the "packages," threw them on the floor, and gruffly said, "Do not fail again."

Yamato and Itsuki left and walked the six blocks to the Japanese Hospital.

Nurse Aikawa saw the river of blood flowing down their raised hands onto the floor. She knew that these *orokamono* (idiots) either hadn't taken care of their wounds or they fucked up again and had to cut off another chunk of their fingers.

"Back again?" She said.

"We need to see the doctor," Itsuki said.

Aikawa looked at the two losers standing bleeding on the floor and said, "No shit. Have a seat over there and try not to bleed everywhere."

Under his breath, Yamato uttered, "*Meinu* (bitch)."

"What did you call me!" Nurse Aikawa said.

Itsuki quickly tried to de-escalate the tension in the room, "He didn't mean anything. It's just the stress talking."

"Don't fuck with me, cowboy. I'll come over there and cut off something more painful than your God Damn finger. Got it!"

Nurse Aikawa saw action in the war. She and her unit landed on Omaha Beach hours after the initial landing and were assigned to Patton's Third Army. She was awarded the Purple Heart for being wounded during the Battle of the Bulge. When Patton pinned the Purple Heart on her, he winked and whispered, "You, Nurse Aikawa, are one crusty old battle axe, and thank God you were on our side."

A short time passed, and a male nurse entered the waiting room to collect Yamato and Itsuki and bring them back to see the doctor.

He handed each of them a clipboard and said, "Fill these out, and the doctor will be right in."

Yamato turned to Itsuki and asked, "Are you Smith or Jonze?"

"It don't matter," Itsuki replied.

Before they finished completing the forms, Doctor Yamaguchi entered the room. He saw the blood-soaked bandages and knew immediately what had happened.

"Who wants to go first?" He asked.

After examining Yamato's finger, he said, "I'm going to have to cauterize your finger."

"What does that mean? Is it painful?" Yamato asked.

"I'm afraid so," Yamaguchi said.

"Just put a bandage on it," Yamato demanded.

"If I don't cauterize it, you could lose your hand. Is that what you want?"

"I'll take my chances," Yamato said defiantly.

"How about you?" Doctor Yamaguchi asked Itsuki.

"I don't want to lose my hand," Itsuki muttered.

Yamaguchi turned to the nurse and said, "Prepare the probe for cauterization."

The nurse placed the metal probe into a heated pot until the tip glowed bright reddish-orange. Then, he handed the probe to Doctor Yamaguchi.

"Nurse, hold onto the patient's hand, and do not let go. Understand?"

"Yes, Doctor."

Itsuki was seated, and the nurse held tight to Itsuki's hand as Doctor Yamaguchi brought the red-hot probe down onto the infected finger.

"*RAAAAAAAHHHHHH*!!!!!"

The smell of burning flesh filled the room. Both Yamato and Itsuki vomited.

Doctor Yamaguchi said, "Nurse, help Mr. Smith to lie on the table. I'll be back to bandage the wound in a few minutes."

"Yes, doctor."

Itsuki lay down on the examination table; he was as white as a ghost. Yamato, still bleeding, asked, "Hey, sport, do you think you could bandage me up here?"

"Oh, sorry."

While waiting for Doctor Yamaguchi to return, the nurse cleaned Yamato's finger and bandaged it again.

"It will continue bleeding for a couple of hours. If it's still bleeding tomorrow, come back."

"Yeah, right. I'm going to wait out there for him," Yamato said as he left the room.

Doctor Yamaguchi returned, looked at the cauterized wound, and bandaged it.

"It looks good. Just take it easy for a couple of days and come back next week. I'll give you some pills for the pain. If it's still bothering you, come back. Don't be a hero, or you could lose the hand. Understand, Mr. Jonze?"

"It's Mr. Smith."

"Smith. Jonze. Whatever. Do you understand? And be sure to pay on your way out." Yamaguchi said.

"*Hai.*"

Marlboro and Wakabayashi called Detective Tanaka to inform him of their latest run-in with the thugs from Black Rain.

"Hello, Yuki, it's Marlboro. I thought we should call and let you know about those two mugs with the missing fingers. They came back."

"And?" Tanaka asked.

Well, Wakabayashi karate kicked a gun out of one of the jamoke's hands, which allowed me to get the drop on the other punk."

"And?"

"And. We got the name of the big cheese and his lieutenants after we sent them out of here crying. Literally."

"So, who are the bosses?"

"Kio Kobayashi is the main guy. Aoi Yamaguchi, Minato Aoki, and Kenji Yamamoto are the Capos. We haven't gotten the names of the torpedoes yet, other than the two goombahs Yamato and Itsuki," Marlboro said.

"I'll get the boys working on finding out about Kobayashi and his crew. In the meantime, you guys, be careful. I got a feeling they'll be coming at ya hard and fast. So, watch your backs."

"Will do," Marlboro said.

"Good work, Marlboro. Tell Wakabayashi she has done well, too."

Marlboro hung up the phone, smiled, and said, "Tanaka says you done good."

"Anything else?"

"Yeah, shit's going to get real. So, buckle up."

"Just to be safe, let's check all the doors and windows," Wakabayashi said.

"Then we'll get the guns locked and loaded and in place for if and when the shit hits the fan."

54

Chapter Six
The Break In

After they had ensured everything was locked down and secured, Marlboro and Wakabayashi went upstairs to the apartment. It was a modest residence with a tiny kitchen/dining area, a meager living room, a paltry bathroom, and a small one-bedroom, big enough for only a double-sized bed and a runty chest of drawers.

For the past two weeks, Marlboro took to sleeping on the couch in the living room with a loaded 9mm Parabellum Browning machine pistol under his pillow. Before bedding down for the night, he set the store's door and window alarms as well as a couple of homemade booby traps around the apartment. He's had run-ins with organized crime families before, and one could never be too careful.

It was a little after three a.m. when he was awakened by what sounded like someone using a glass cutter on the living room window. He stealthily crawled over to the window and spied two men dressed all in black, wearing matching balaclavas, standing on the fire escape using a glass cutter. Marlboro returned to the couch, retrieved his pistol, sat in the chair facing the window, and waited.

The room was in total darkness; the living room window faced the alley, so there wasn't any light shining in, although there was enough ambient light, so the figures were slightly backlit when they climbed into the room.

Once they were both in, Marlboro reached for the floor lamp and turned it on. Both men looked like deer caught in the headlights.

Pointing his pistol at the men, he said, "Get down on your knees slowly and put your hands inside your pockets. Try anything, and the two of you will be wearing a couple of Chicago overcoats."

Once they complied, Marlboro hollered, "Oh, Aiko, come look. We've got a couple of unexpected guests."

Wakabayashi eased out of the bedroom, wearing A full-length green silk brocade Japanese Kimono. Her hand was in the pocket, gripping a .32 caliber Colt Detective Special 'snub-nosed' revolver.

"Oh, Butch, what a pleasant surprise. You must introduce me."

"Okay, dear. I will," Marlboro said, moving behind the two men. He placed his pistol on the back of the first man, patted him down, and found that he had a Colt—Police .38 Special equipped with a silencer and a *tantō*. The second man had exactly the same weaponry.

"Tisk-tisk. That is not what I would expect from neighbors. Would you, dear?" Marlboro asked Wakabayashi.

"I didn't realize that we moved into such a rough neighborhood," She said sarcastically.

Marlboro tapped the first man on the head with his pistol and asked, "What's your name, friend?"

The man said nothing.

Marlboro pulled the balaclava off his head and cocked the pistol, placing it on the man's head.

"I'll ask you one more time. What's your name?"

The man remained silent.

"Okay," Marlboro aimed the gun and shot the man in the back of the thigh.

KAPOW!

The man let out a scream and fell forward onto the floor, withering in pain.

"*AAIEEEEEHHHH!*"

Marlboro moved to the second man, ripped his balaclava off, placed the gun to his head, and asked, "What is your name?"

The villain that was shot uttered, "*Damare* (shut up)!"

Marlboro cocked the pistol and asked, "What is your name?"

The man answered, "Haruto."

"And your friend?"

"Riku."

"Who do you work for?"

Riku shouted, "*Damare* (shut up)!"

Marlboro walked over to Riku and stomped on his leg, causing him to scream out.

"*AAIEEEEEHHHH!*"

Pointing his pistol at Haruto's leg, Marlboro asked, "Who do you work for?"

Haruto didn't hesitate, "*Kuroi Ame* (Black Rain)."

"Now, was that so hard," Marlboro said, smiling.

Marlboro called to Wakabayashi and asked, "Honey, would you mind calling the police? And be sure to ask for an ambulance for our friend, Riku."

Wakabayashi picked up the receiver and dialed the number of Detective Tanaka.

"Hello, police; this is Aiko Baker. Sorry to call you so late, but we've captured a couple of intruders in our apartment.

Could you send some officers and an ambulance? One of the prowlers has been shot."

"Tanaka asked, "Are you all right?""

"Yes, we're fine."

"Hang tight. I'm on my way with the calvary," Tanaka said.

Wakabayashi placed the receiver down and said, "Butch, the police said they'd be right over."

"That's great. Do me a favor, doll, and get me a rag to try and stop this *panko* (punk) from bleeding all over our rug."

Detective Tanaka arrived at the same time as the ambulance and the two squad cars. A large crowd had amassed on the street, gawking and rubber-necking to see what all the hubbub was about. Two familiar faces, Yamato and Itsuki, stood in the shadows, watching intently. They were overjoyed when they saw Haruto being led out in handcuffs and Riku carried out on a stretcher.

"See, Itsuki, at least we didn't get arrested or shot."

"Yeah, we must be looking pretty good to the *oyabun* right about now," Itsuki said.

"So, what happened, Marlboro?" Tanaka asked.

"Well, I was sacked out on the sofa when I heard some scratching at the living room window. I eased over and saw a couple of brunos dressed all in black, wearing balaclavas. I grabbed my roscoe, sat on that chair, and waited. Once inside, I flipped on the light switch and got the drop on them."

"How did the perp get shot in the leg?"

"I was questioning them when this mug suddenly started to tap dance around, so I plugged him," Marlboro explained.

"Officer Wakabayashi, did you witness this?" Tanaka asked.

"No, sir. I hadn't come out from the bedroom yet."

Marlboro had instructed Wakabayashi to say she didn't see the shooting to avoid getting her into trouble as a possible accessory if things got hinky.

"That guy you shot is claiming that you stomped on his leg. Is that true?"

"Aw, come on. You know me, would I do something like that? I must have tripped over him. He was wiggling all over the floor and crying like a baby."

"I see. Wakabayashi, did you see that happened?"

"Yeah, Sarge. The perp was spazzing out all over the floor, and Marlboro accidentally stepped on the guy's leg."

"You know I don't give a flying spondulix one way or the other. But I have to ask. Okay, you do know that the Black Rain is going to get more aggressive," Tanaka warned.

"What have you discovered about this guy Kobayashi and his goons?" Marlboro asked.

"Kio Kobayashi is originally from Tokyo. He is part of Japan's third-largest yakuza group, the *Inagawa-kai* clan. Founded in 1949, they were the first of the yakuza organizations to begin operating overseas."

"Lucky us," Marlboro quipped.

"Kobayashi was their fair-haired boy hand-picked to establish a foothold in America, bringing extortion, gambling, drugs, and prostitution. He brought along his lieutenants Aoi Yamaguchi, Minato Aoki, and Kenji Yamamoto with him. They have several henchmen, four of whom you've already had the pleasure of meeting. Yamato and Itsuki were first, and now these two, Haruto and Riku. They all have extensive criminal records in Japan, and now they're building up their resumes here in the States," Tanaka said.

"Any idea how many gunsels the Black Rain have on the payroll?" Wakabayashi asked.

"We're not sure, but I would imagine at least another dozen or so."

"Great. It's starting to feel like Fort Apache around here," Marlboro said.`

"You know, you guys can call the whole thing off. Just say the word," Tanaka said.

"No way. I love a good Western. The good guys battling the bad guys, it's as American as apple pie, John Wayne, and Tail O' the Pup hot dogs," Marlboro said.

"What about you, Officer Wakabayashi?" Tanaka asked.

"I like apple pie," She said.

"Okay, then. Keep me posted. I'll try to have more undercover cops in the area and black and whites cruising more often."

"Detective," Marlboro said.

"Yeah?"

"I thought you might want these," Marlboro said as he handed Tanaka the two Colt – Police .38 Specials and the two *tantōs*.

"Thanks for the souvenirs."

"See ya," Marlboro said.

"Stay frosty, you two," Tanaka said as he left.

Chapter Seven
The Finger

Kio Kobayashi sat with his lieutenants seated silently on either side of him, no one daring to speak first. Kobayashi's eyes were closed as he transcended into another astral plane; he was becoming one with his samurai ancestors in a moment of Zen. Soon, the path forward became apparent; he would send his most deadly warrior, Ichiro, to dispatch these troublesome shop owners once and for all.

"Ichiro, you are my most trusted samurai. I want you to eliminate this malignant growth that has sprung up here within our territory. If they succeed, then others may follow and refuse to comply. We cannot abide that to happen. Now, go and bring me back their heads!" Kobayashi ordered.

"*Hai masutā* (yes, master)," Ichiro said as he bowed.

Once the word got out that the paint store owners had put up resistance and had two of the Black Rain arrested, people started thinking that they, too, might resist. So, the Little Tokyo Council members decided to call another town hall meeting with Detective Sergeant Tanaka and special guest speakers Butch and Aiko Baker before someone got hurt.

Council President Botan Ito and the entire city council were in attendance. Sitting in the back of the meeting room were Detective Jeffery Juneau and Detective Charlie Bell on opposite sides so as not to draw too much attention to themselves. The room was packed with the local shop owners just itching to hear about the Baker's encounters with the Black Rain. Two figures dressed incognito were seated in the very back; they were no other than Yamato and Itsuki.

President Botan Ito stepped up to the podium and said, "*Kon'nichiwa*. Hello, and greetings. I want to thank you all for coming out tonight. Before we hear from Butch and Akio Baker from the *Natsukashī Kokoro* paint store, I thought it best to hear from Detective Sergeant Tanaka from the LAPD.

The audience gave a polite smattering of applause when Detective Tanaka stood to speak.

"*Arigatō*. Thank you. I'm glad to see so many shop owners here tonight. Before I turn the microphone over to Butch and Aiko, I want to reiterate that what they did isn't something that we in the police department suggest that the average citizen try and do. The Bakers will tell you about their many years of training and experience in karate and hand-to-hand combat. So, I urge you all to pay close attention to what they have to say.

Now are there any questions you might have before I turn things over to Butch and Aiko?"

There were no questions. When Marlboro and Wakabayashi stood to speak, the crowd went wild, clapping, whistling, and cheering. The crowd seemed to have come to see two Hollywood movie stars. As Marlboro walked up to the podium, he recognized Yamato and Itsuki, dressed in shabby clothes, wearing glasses and straw trilby fedora hats.

Marlboro raised his hands to quiet the people down before speaking, "*Kon'nichiwa*."

The audience went nuts. They jumped up and gave Marlboro and Wakabayashi a standing ovation for over ten minutes.

Finally, Marlboro said, "*Arigatō*. Thank you. Please have a seat. Please."

The crowd eventually settled down and took their seats. Marlboro began to speak once silence had been achieved.

"Good evening, everyone. Akio and I want to thank you for your warm welcome. We are proud to be members of the Little Tokyo community.

Now, I want to echo Detective Tanaka's earlier words about Aiko's years of karate experience and my training and fighting Nazis in hand-to-hand combat. So, I urge you not to take on any of these yakuza goons unless you have many years of training. You'll be going up against professionals who would rather slit your throat than look at you. So, please, please do not try to use a gun; most people are killed by their own weapons."

Wakabayashi walked up to stand next to Marlboro at the podium.

She smiled her kewpie doll smile and said, "*Kon'nichiwa*. I'm Akio Baker. Butch and I own the *Natsukashī Kokoro*. As Butch said, we've both had many years of experience. I'm a black belt in karate, and Butch has a decorated war veteran and instructor in hand-to-hand combat. We ask you all not to engage with these punks from Black Rain. Report any threats and extortion to the police and let them handle things. We need you all to stand together," Wakabayashi said.

A hand shot up from the back of the room. Chikao Sasaki, the owner of the Mikado Market, stood and asked, "Mr. Butch, question. Is it true that you shot one of the enforcers?"

"I did. However, it was after he and another man broke into our apartment late last night," Marlboro said.

"Did you kill him?"

"No. I happened to shoot him in the leg."

"Are you and Akio afraid?" Sasaki asked.

"I wouldn't say that we're afraid, but we are cautious."

The back doors swung open with such force that it created a commotion, and everyone turned around to see what had caused it. Wearing wraparound sunglasses and a thousand-dollar sharkskin suit, Ichiro stood in the doorway looking menacing.

Marlboro could tell even from where he stood, at least a hundred feet away, that Ichiro was packing heat in a shoulder holster.

The samurai warrior put his hand inside his coat pocket and withdrew several *shurikens* (throwing stars). Then, with pinpoint accuracy, he flicked four stars at Marlboro, who anticipated what was coming his way. He picked up a wooden clipboard and held it up to cover his face.

THAWACK! THAWACK! THAWACK! THAWACK!

All four would have hit their intended mark if it had not been for Marlboro's quick thinking. The people in attendance panicked and ran out of the community center's meeting room helter-skelter.

Seeing that his target outwitted him, Ichiro drew his Walther PPK pistol from his shoulder holster and methodically began walking toward Wakabayashi and Marlboro. When he reached within fifty feet, he stopped and raised his pistol. Marlboro had seen Ichiro had pulled a revolver; he wasted no time; he instinctively withdrew the 9mm Parabellum Browning machine pistol he had tucked in his waistband.

Because of all the chaos, Ichiro didn't see that Marlboro was armed. Officer Wakabayashi and Detective Tanaka were in the process of drawing their weapons when Ichiro fired one shot, missing Marlboro, who feigned to his left while firing off two shots, the second one grazing Ichiro on the right side of his head, spinning him around and knocking him down.

KAPOW! KAPOW! KAPOW

Detective Juneau and Detective Bell, held up by the stampede of the people running out of the building, finally arrived to place the unconscious Ichiro in handcuffs. All the while, Yamato and Itsuki stood in the back of the room agog at what had just happened. Ichiro was Black Rain's number one. Now, three top *heitals* (soldiers) were injured and in custody. The *oyabun* isn't going to be happy.

"Whose going to tell Kobayashi?" Itsuki asked.

"I say we let him read it in the papers," Yamato said.

Kobayashi's face gnarled and turned a scarlet red, his eyes twined in anger, and one would swear that steam bellowed from his ears when he screamed, "*Kuso ttare* (Goddamnit)!" as he pounded on the mahogany *chabudai.*

He turned to his lieutenants and snarled, "I want to know who this Butch Baker and his wife Aiko are. I want to know everything about them. Understand?"

Aoi Yamaguchi, the Black Rain's number two, secretly wants Kobayashi to fail so he can take over the reins.

"Kobayashi-san, should we request more *koroshi-ya* (hitmen) from Tokyo?" Yamaguchi asked.

Kobayashi stared at Yamaguchi with hatred and said, "Go and bail out Haruto, Riku, and, if possible, Ichiro."

"Now?"

"*Hai, ima* (yes, now)!" Kobayashi barked as he slammed his fist on the table.

Yamaguchi left the conference room thinking that all it would take was for Kobayashi to screw up one more time, and he would be ousted.

"Yeah, what do you want?" Officer O'Reilly, the Little Tokyo precinct desk sergeant, asked.

"I would like to post bail for Haruto Sugimoto, Riku Usui, and Ichiro Hamaguchi."

"And you would be?"

"I am Aoi Yamaguchi."

"Yeah. And you would be?"

Looking confused, Yamaguchi once again said, "I am Aoi Yamaguchi."

"We got that. Are you their lawyer, their brother, their sister? Who are you?" O'Reilly said, getting frustrated.

"Ah so. I am their employer."

"And what do you do?"

"I am in the savings and loan business."

"What is the name of your company?

"Yamaguchi Holdings."

O'Reilly knew this guy was blowing smoke up his ass with this whole Yamaguchi Holdings bullshit. This Jap bastard was a loan shark, if ever there was one. O'Reilly reached into one of the desk drawers and pulled out several forms this Yamaguchi creep needed to fill out.

"Here you go. Haruto Sugimoto and Riku Usui are available for bail. Ichiro Hamaguchi is not; he's in the infirmary. You need to fill out these forms and bring them back filled out along with the bail money," O'Reilly said.

"How much is the bail?"

"That you will find out when you go to the court clerk's office upstairs," O'Reilly said, pointing to the staircase to his left.

Yamaguchi trudged up the stairs to the court clerk's office. There, he was informed that bail had been set for Haruto and Riku at ten thousand dollars each.

The woman behind the counter, who was reading the latest edition of the National Enquirer, appeared to be bored with the drudgery of her civil servant's job, showed no astonishment when Yamaguchi reached into his coat pocket, withdrew twenty thousand in cash, and plopped it down on the counter.

She nonchalantly swooped up the cash and proceeded to fast-count it. Then, she picked up her rubber stamp and marked the bail request 'Paid in Full.'

She picked up her National Enquirer and said, "Take this back downstairs and give it to the desk sergeant. "

"Yeah, what do you want?" Officer O'Reilly asked.

"I have posted bail for Haruto Sugimoto and Riku Usui."

"Have a seat over there, and I'll call you when they're released. O'Reilly said.

Yamaguchi waited for over an hour before Haruto and Riku were released.

When they came waltzing out from the jail, Haruto was walking with a cane, having been shot in the thigh. Yamaguchi, as well as Haruto and Riku, knew what awaited them.

When they returned to the conference room, Kobayashi and his lieutenants were taking, drinking sake and eating sushi. The room became quiet when they entered.

Unmoved by Haruto's injury, Kobayashi looked at Yamaguchi and said, "Where is Ichiro?"

"He is in the jail's infirmary and could not be released," Yamaguchi answered.

Haruto and Riku saw three pieces of kasuri cloth at the end of the table. The lieutenants and Kobayashi sat stoically, waiting for the two incompetents to take their places at the far end of the table.

After they were seated, Haruto bowed his head and said, "*Oyabun*, I humbly ask…"

Kobayashi cut him off. "Silence. You and Riku have brought shame and dishonor to your clan. There is no excuse. You know that you must atone for your failure. It is the way of the *Bushido* Code. It is the way of the warrior," He said as he slid two *tantōs* toward Haruto and Riku. And just like Yamato and Itsuki, they each took the sword in their right hand, unsheathed the *tantō*, and placed the weapon carefully in front of them.

"*Yubitsume!*" Kobayashi ordered.

They each took the sword in their right hand, unsheathed the blade, and placed the weapon carefully in front of them.

"*Yubitsume!*" Kobayashi growled.

As Yamato and Itsuki before them, they bowed, then placed their left hand face down on the small *kasuri* cloth; they Picked up the weapon and off a portion of their left little finger.

Afterward, they tied off the bleeding stump, wrapped the severed portion of their finger in the *kasuri* cloth, and submitted the "package" to Kobayashi.

Everyone seated around the table had committed *yubitsume* at least once. If you're willing to join the yakuza, you knew there might come a time when you would be required to execute *yubitsume*.

"Haruto, when will you be able to take on another assignment?" Kobayashi asked.

"The doctor said, probably next week, *oyabun*."

"Good. Now, you both may go."

Once Haruto and Riku left, Kobayashi called *Tadaaki* (faithful light) his dog, a hundred-thirty-pound Akita, a breed that originated in the mountainous regions of Japan, to sit beside him. He dropped the fragments of the severed fingers onto the mahogany *chabudai,* where *Tadaaki* crunched the digits with gusto.

Marlboro and Wakabayashi closed up the paint store early and walked the two blocks to the *Kawafuku* Restaurant—a favorite amongst the local population.

"I must tell you, I've never eaten raw fish before, doll. The whole idea sounds disgusting," Marlboro said.

"They have other things other than sushi. You know, for a tough guy, you sure are a baby."

"Maybe I'll have the chop suey."

"That's Chinese."

"Do you think they would have bossy in a bowl?"

"What the Hell is that? Never mind, I don't even want to know. Just try not to embarrass me," Wakabayashi said.

The hostess wore her hair in the traditional Shimada mage style and wore a beautiful silk kimono. She gathered two menus, bowed slightly, and said, "*Konbanwa* (good evening)."

Wakabayashi smiled, bowed, and said, "two-*Ri-yō no seki* (table for two)."

They were shown to a private tatami room decorated with sliding doors, unique Japanese flower arrangements, scrolls, and artwork. At the chabudai table, there were thick pillows to sit on. Wakabayashi removed her shoes before sitting down, and Marlboro followed suit.

The hostess handed them their menus and asked, "*Saké*?"

"Yes, please," Marlboro said enthusiastically.

When the hostess left, Wakabayashi and Marlboro began to scan the menu.

"So, what looks good to you?" Wakabayashi asked.

"Mmm, I don't know. It all looks so good," Marlboro answered with a slight bite of sarcasm.

An equally beautiful waitress dressed in a traditional Japanese outfit brought the warm *sake* in a *tokkuri* (sake bottle) with two *ochokos* (small ceramic cups) and placed them on the table. She then poured sake into each cup. Afterward, she asked, "Good evening, my name is Kaori. I'll be your server tonight. Have you decided?"

Marlboro gestured for Wakabayashi to go first.

"Yes, I'll have the Maguro Sashimi (sliced raw tuna) for my appetizer. And for my entrée, I'll have the *Nikuyasai* (pork and vegetables)."

"And for you, sir?" She asked Marlboro.

"I'll start with the *Ikano Shiokara* (marinated squid). And for my entrée, I'll go with the *Tako Sumiso* (octopus with miso sauce)," Marlboro said in near-perfect Japanese.

Kaori gave a slight bow and said, "*Arigatō*."

Wakabayashi gave Marlboro a look of dubiety. She leaned forward and said, "I thought you said you had never eaten Japanese."

Marlboro sheepishly smiled and said, "I lied."

On the walk back to the paint store, Marlboro noticed they were being followed. He said to Wakabayashi, "Why don't we stop so you can fix your makeup."

"Is there something wrong with my makeup?" She asked.

"No. Just check it and see if you spot a mug following us. He's wearing a black motorcycle jacket, about six feet tall, and aviator glasses."

They stopped, and she took out her compact and pretended to put on lipstick. Looking in her mirror, she saw the guy Marlboro had mentioned.

"Yep, I see him. He's about a block behind us. What do you want to do?" Wakabayashi asked.

"Let's just keep strolling back to the store and hunker in. Are you packing?"

"Yeah. Got my .38."

"I don't think he'd try anything on the street. Just stay sharp," Marlboro said.

When they arrived at the paint store, Marlboro locked the door. He told Wakabayashi to go into the backroom while he stayed in the main area, pretending to be doing inventory.

It wasn't long before the man in the black leather jacket stood outside the store and knocked on the door.

"We're closed. Comeback tomorrow," Marlboro said.

"The stranger looked around to be sure he wasn't being observed. When he felt it was okay, he flashed his LAPD badge.

Marlboro unlocked the door and let the man in. He shouted to Wakabayashi, "Wakabayashi, come on in here; we have a visitor."

Wakabayashi emerged from the backroom, holding her pistol at the ready.

"Good evening. I'm Officer Goro Miake; Detective Tanaka suggested I keep an eye on you. So, I thought I'd come by and introduce myself."

"Well, we appreciate that. Come on in. Would you like some coffee or tea?" Marlboro asked.

"Sure, I never refuse a good cup of Joe," Miake said.

Marlboro smiled and said, "Hey, I never said it was good."

The three of them went upstairs to the apartment. Wakabayashi stepped into the kitchen to put the coffee pot on. Miake and Marlboro sat opposite each other at the small dining room table.

"So, how long have you worked with Detective Tanaka?" Marlboro asked.

"Not long, I just transferred in from the Valley."

"Where, Van Nuys? What's that, the twenty-first precinct?"

"Yeah," Miake said.

"Been a cop long? You look like you're not even old enough to drive," Marlboro laughed.

Wakabayashi brought out three cups of coffee, cream, and sugar and placed them in the center of the table.

"Help yourself. Hope you like it," Wakabayashi said.

As Miake reached for his cup of coffee, he leaned down, as if he were about to scratch his ankle.

Marlboro raised his semi-automatic Colt M1911 .45 caliber pistol and pointed it at Miake.

"Stop right there. Ease that gat right on up and gingerly place it on the table. Any sudden moves, and I'll spatter your brains all over the wall," Marlboro said.

"What, are you crazy? Miake asked.

"Just lay the gun on the table, now," Marlboro said as he cocked the .45.

Miake did as he was told. He removed the .38 snub-nosed pistol from his ankle holster and laid it on the table.

"What gave me away, *gaijin*?" Miake sneered.

"Well, for one thing, Van Nuys is the ninth precinct, not the twenty-first; the badge that you flashed wasn't an LAPD badge; it looked like you got it from the Woolworths, and the fact that you're missing part of your left finger was a major red flag, ya big palooka. Now, slide out of that chair and get your ass on the floor."

Once he was lying on the floor, Marlboro frisked him and found that he was carrying several throwing stars as well as a *Tantō*.

"Hey, Aiko, be a doll and do me a favor. Can you call Miake's old amigo Detective Tanaka?" Marlboro asked Wakabayashi as he placed Miake in handcuffs.

"Detective Tanaka, sorry to bother you. But we have another button man captured in our apartment.

No, we're both fine. It might be best if you come in a black and white. Why? Well, this one posed as a cop, and we'd feel more secure you're with them.

Okay, we'll see you soon." Wakabayashi said.

Twenty minutes later, Tanaka showed up at their door.

"Well. Well. Well. If it isn't Goro Miake," Detective Tanaka said as he walked into the apartment above the paint store.

"You know this goon?" Marlboro asked.

"Oh, yeah, Goro and I are old friends. Aren't we?"

"*Fakkuyū* (fuck you)!" Miake sneered.

"Nice talk. Do you kiss your mother with that mouth?"

"*Rokudenashi* (bastard)."

"So, what did this mastermind do, Mr. Baker?" Tanaka asked.

"We spot this mug tailing us from *Kawafuku* Restaurant. So, when we get inside, he taps on the door and flashes this badge. Well, I can tell right away that it's bogus. That's strike one. He tells me that you have him watching over us. So, I let him in and invited him here for some coffee.

While Aiko is making us some coffee, we get to talking. He tells me he has transferred from Van Nuys' twenty-first prescient. That, to me, is strike two, but you know what the real clincher was?"

"The finger?"

"The finger. Strike three. You're out. While he's edging down to grab his gat from his ankle holster, I get the drop on him, and here we are," Marlboro said.

"You are very resourceful, Mr. Baker."

"Butch, please."

"Well, Butch, I have to take my hat off to you and the Misses. I wish all our Little Tokyo citizens were as savvy as you two."

"Why, thank you, Detective Tanaka. Coming from you, that really is a compliment," Marlboro said with a wink.

"Now, Butch, Aiko, we're going to take this varmint on down to the jail and book 'em. You can come down at your convenience and lodge a complaint," Tanaka said.

Tanaka turned to one of the uniforms and said, "Take this creep down and book him."

"Yes, sir," The officer said.

Once Miake was taken away, Tanaka asked, "Are you two sure you want to continue?"

Marlboro looked at Wakabayashi and said, "Whatta think, doll?"

"I'm good," She said.

"Next time, they're going to come all out. I'm sure that Kobayashi will want to make an example of you. Wakabayashi, are you prepared to do what it takes? I know Marlboro is he's one crazy bastard, but are you?" Tanaka asked.

"Hey, I'm right here. I can hear you," Marlboro said.

"Like I said, Marlboro is one crazy bastard. I'm concerned about you, Hana. It would help if you didn't feel pressured. I'm sure Marlboro is willing to carry on by himself if you decide this isn't for you. No one will think any the less of you," Tanaka said.

Wakabayashi thought for a while, then answered, "I'll stick it out, sir."

"Okay. Call me if you need anything," Tanaka said as he left.

"I'll walk you out," Marlboro said.

Marlboro smiled when they reached the front door and said, "Don't worry about Wakabayashi; she's one tough cookie. I won't let anything bad happen to her."

"I know."

Marlboro locked the door and headed back upstairs, where he found Wakabayashi standing in the bedroom doorway wearing her kimono. It was open, revealing that she was naked underneath.

"*Beddo ni kite* (come to bed), Marlboro," She whispered as she let the silk robe drop to the floor.

When Marlboro woke up the following day, Wakabayashi was still asleep. He watched her sleep for twenty minutes. Laying there, she looked so angelic and peaceful that he didn't want to wake her. Marlboro got dressed and checked his Timex; it was 6 a.m. He decided to go out for some coffee and donuts to bring back to the apartment.

He walked the four blocks to *Misutādōnatsu* (Mister Donut) for two black coffees and four plain glazed donuts as he had done daily since he and Wakabayashi had opened *Natsukashī Kokoro*.

Fuji Ogawa, the owner of *Misutādōnatsu,* had just removed six trays of fresh glazed donuts from the oven when Marlboro entered the shop.

"*Ohayō* (good morning), Ogawa-san."

"*Ohayō*, Butch-san," Mister Ogawa said.

"Two coffees, black and four plain glazed donuts, and an L.A. Times, please."

As Ogawa bagged the order, Marlboro gazed out the shop's large plate glass window. He spotted Yamato and Itsuki casually strolling towards the donut shop. Marlboro asked Ogawa, " May I use the restroom, Ogawa-san?"

"Yes, of course."

Marlboro stepped into the bathroom, keeping the door cracked so he could hear what Yamato and Itsuki were up to.

"Fuji-san!" Yamato roared.

"What can I do you for?" Ogawa asked.

"Did you hear that, Itsuki? Fuji-san wants to know what he can do for us," Yamato said sarcastically.

"Fuji-san, he's one funny guy, Yamato," Itsuki said, laughing.

"We're here for the protection payment, *baka* (fool). Don't play dumb," Yamato said, pointing a .38 pistol at *Misutādōnatsu*.

"Hey, boys. What are you up to?" Marlboro asked, holding a Semi-automatic Colt M1911 .45 caliber by his side.

Marlboro could see Yamato considering a gunfight with him, the man who forced him to commit two acts of *yubitsume* that cost him two knuckles from his left hand.

Itsuki pulled back his jacket to reveal a pistol tucked into the waistband of his pants.

"Even if you boys tie me, you're both dead," Marlboro said as he raised his Colt.

Yamato and Itsuki thought that if it got back to Kobayashi, this despicable *gaijin* bested them again; losing another knuckle would be the least they would lose.

The moment Yamato started to turn and Itsuki began to reach for his piece, Marlboro fired off eight shots, killing both Yamato and Itsuki and splattering blood and brains all over Mister Donuts' plate glass windows.

Once the shooting started, the owner of *Misutādōnatsu* ducked below the counter. Afterward, Marlboro could hear him whimpering.

"Ogawa-san, you can come up now. Would you please call the police?" Marlboro calmly asked.

In less than ten minutes, *Misutādōnatsu* was surrounded by eight LAPD black and whites, three network news trucks, four reporters, and two photographers from the Los Angeles Times. News networks love nothing more than multiple homicides. Their motto is "If it bleeds, it leads."

Once the cameras were set up, twelve of LA.'s finest came storming into Mister Donut, weapons drawn. When they entered the donut shop, they found Marlboro, his hands raised, his Colt M1911 .45 caliber lying on the counter, and two Black Rain gang members dead on the floor.

While being interviewed, Marlboro noticed Kio Kobayashi among the crowd gathered outside watching the proceedings. Detective Sergeant Tanaka and the medical examiner arrived shortly after the uniforms and media circus arrived.

"What happened, Mr. Baker?" Tanaka asked.

"Well, Detective, I came to Mister Donut like I always do for my morning coffee and donuts. While Mr. Ogawa was getting my order ready, I went to use the bathroom. When I came out, I saw these two men holding a gun on Mr. Ogawa, demanding money. When they noticed me, they pointed the gun toward me. I feared for my life and was lucky to get the drop on them." Marlboro explained.

"Is that what happened, Mr. Ogawa?" Tanaka asked.

"Detective Tanaka-san, I am but an old man. I do not wish to get involved."

"Two men were shot to death in your shop. You are involved. Now, tell me, Mr. Ogawa, what happened?" Tanaka demanded.

Ogawa began to hem and haw when pressed.

"Well, it happened so fast," He said.

"Did one of these men pull a gun on you, yes or no?" Tanaka asked, pointing to Yamato and Itsuki lying on the floor.

He hesitantly answered, "Yes."

"Which one?"

"Yamato," Ogawa said, pointing at the dead man.

"I'll need you to come downtown to get a statement, Mr. Baker."

"Gladly, Detective," Marlboro said.

Tanaka turned to Ogawa and said, "At some point, I'll need you to come down to the station to give a statement, as well, Mr. Ogawa."

The medical examiner was going through the deceased's pockets and placing the items into an evidence bag.

Doctor Gyening, the M.E., chuckled and asked Tanaka, "Do you want to know the cause of death?"

"You're a real funny guy, Doc. Almost as funny as a broken leg. Come on, Mr. Baker, let's go," Tanaka said.

When they walked outside, they were engulfed in a swarm of reporters, photographers, and newsmen with microphones yelling and screaming questions as Marlboro and Tanaka made their way to Tanaka's squad car.

"What happened?"

"No comment."

"Was it robbery?"

"No comment."
"Is this the shooter?"
"No comment."
"Who were the victims?"
"No comment."
"How many were shot?"
"No comment."
"Come on, Detective, say something."
"Okay. No comment."

Chapter Eight
Banzai

When hearing of Goro Miake's failure and arrest and the now killing of Yamato and Itsuki, Kobayashi could not control his rage. He pounded his fists so hard that he splintered the top of the *chabudai* as he screamed, "Whose idea was having Goro Miake impersonate the police!"

Minato Aoki, the number three man, bowed and admitted, "*Oyabun*, it was me. It is a tactic we had successfully used in the past."

"Why did you not ask my permission, Aoki?" Kobayashi asked.

Aoki sat silent, head bowed.

Kobayashi said, "Because you wanted to show initiative. Is that not right?"

"*Hai.*"

Kobayashi reached under the *chabudai* and withdrew a *kasuri* cloth and a *tantō*. He slid both over to Number Three and grunted, "*Yubitsume!*"

Aoki picked up the *tantō* and slowly began to cut off a portion of his left little finger above the top knuckle of the finger. The crackling and crunching of the distal phalanges as the sword's blade cut through the bone made him vomit onto his bleeding wound and then passed out.

When Aoki regained consciousness, he saw Kobayashi feeding his amputated digit to *Tadaaki,* his dog. The *oyabun* stared down at Aoki with disdain and coldly snarled, "*Koshinuke* (coward)!

You are not worthy to be seated with us. From now on, you will take *Tadaaki* for his walks and pick up his *tawagoto* (shit)! Now go!"

Aoki slinked out of the room with *Tadaaki* licking the trail of blood oozing from his unwrapped wound.

Number Two, Aoi Yamaguchi, decided it would be advantageous to pile onto the now disgraced Number Three by suggesting that Aoki was responsible for Yamato and Itsuki's deaths.

"It's too bad that Aoki sent Yamato and Itsuki to *Misutādōnatsu* this morning," Yamaguchi said.

"Is that true?" Kobayashi asked.

"*Hai.*"

The *oyabun* turned to Kenji Yamamoto, the Number Four, and asked, "Do you want to move up to Number Three?"

"*Hai, oyabun.*"

Kobayashi picked up the *tantō* and slid it toward Yamamoto. "Here, you know what you must do."

Picking up the short sword, he answered, "*Hai.*"

"So, what really happened?" Tanaka asked.

"I told you. I was buying donuts and coffee when I spotted Yamato and Itsuki crossing the street, heading toward the donut shop. I asked Ogawa to use the restroom and stayed there with the door cracked so I could hear what was happening." Marlboro explained.

"And? What did you hear?"

"Yamato said that they were there for the protection payment. That's when I came out and confronted the two of them."

"Did you have your weapon out?"

Marlboro lied, "No."

"Then what?"

"I saw Yamato pointing his gun at the old man. I asked, "What are you up to?" That's when Yamato pointed the gun at me. Itsuki slid back his jacket to show me he was packing, too."

"Is that when you drew your gun?"

"Not yet; I saw that they were contemplating their next move. While they were thinking things over, that's when I eased my pistol out and said that even if they tied me, they would both be dead. I guess they thought it was a challenge and decided to go all Kamakazi on me."

"You know the boys downtown aren't going to like this," Tanaka said.

"Bullshit. They knew that this sort of thing would get messy. They want to drive these yakuza punks out of Little Tokyo. Calling in the cops would only complicate matters; that's why they wanted a gunfighter to clean up Dodge. And once the mission is accomplished, they'll kick me to the curb. You know it, and I know it," Marlboro said.

"Then why do it?"

"It's what I do, man."

When Minato Aoki finished walking Kobayashi's dog, *Tadaaki,* he returned him to the *oyabun's* house on Garey Street, just west of East Second Street.

Kobayashi's house looked like a mini fortress. It was surrounded by a ten-foot brick wall topped with barbed wire and a louver privacy-security gate built with angled vertical panels. Two armed guardsmen stood inside and outside the driveway gate.

By the time Aoki deposited *Tadaaki,* the sun dipped below the Pacific, sliding Little Tokyo into darkness. As he walked back to his apartment next to the Santa Monica Fish

Market, he had an eerie sense of doom and that he was being followed. Every time he would stop and turn around, he found no one was there. When he reached his apartment building, out front waiting for him was friend Number Four, Kenji Yamamoto.

"Kenji-san?"

"Ah, Minato-san. How are you?" Yamamoto asked.

"Not good."

"How is your hand?" Yamamoto asked, seeing that the wound had stopped bleeding but looked like it had been caught in a meat grinder.

"Agh, that *kuso* (fucking) dog wouldn't stop chewing on it!"

"You should go see a doctor."

"*Kutabare* (fuck it). Kenji-san, what are you doing here? Did Kobayashi send you here?" Asked Aoki.

"No. I just came by to see how you are doing. I thought that you might need some company and a stiff drink," Yamamoto said as he held up a bottle of Johnny Walker Blue Label.

"Kenji-san, you are a *yoi tomodachi* (good friend). Please come on up," Aoki said as he opened the lobby door.

The interior design of Aoki's apartment was traditional minimalist Japanese decor. The living room floor was covered with tatami mats, and in the center was a forty-eight-inch-long pine *chabudai* surrounded by six zabuton cushions. A five-foot Forestier bamboo floor lamp stood in one corner, and in the opposite corner was a tall Japanese antique vase. On the wall was Hiroshi Yoshida's *Fuji from Kawaguchi Lake*.

When Yamamoto saw the Hiroshi Yoshida painting, his jaw dropped.

"Minato-san, is that a copy?" Yamamoto asked, pointing at the wall.

"Original," Aoki said nonchalantly as he went into the kitchen to get a couple of glasses. When he returned, Yamamoto stood in the middle of the room, staring at *Fuji from Kawaguchi Lake*.

Aoki put the glasses on the *chabudai* and sat on a zabuton cushion. He picked up the bottle of scotch and poured two generous helpings.

"Kenji-san, please sit," Aoki said as he held up a glass.

Yamamoto took the glass of Johnny Walker Blue Label and sat opposite Aoki. He held up his glass to make a toast and said, "*Kanpai* (cheers)."

"*Kanpai.*"

They drank late into the night until Aoki finally passed out from exhaustion and the loss of blood. Yamamoto stood from the *chabudai*; he took his glass into the kitchen, washed it, and placed it back into the cupboard. He then got a rag and began wiping any surface he might have touched to remove any trace of his fingerprints. Once that was done, he removed the *tantō* that he had hidden in his waistband and jammed the short sword's blade deep into Minato Aoki's chest, killing him instantly.

Before leaving, he trashed the apartment to make it look like a robbery. He took Hiroshi Yoshida's Fuji from Kawaguchi Lake off the wall on his way out. He brought it home to his wife, Tsumugi, as a belated anniversary gift.

Tsumugi was so touched by such an expensive gift that that night, she gave Kenji *kōnaiseikō* (oral sex). Afterward, Kenji fell asleep and slept the sleep of the angels.

Kobayashi called a meeting of the Black Rain's *Kanri* (top-level management). He needed to bring in more muscle for a show of force. He was tired of fucking around with this paint store *gaijin*. With the deaths of Yamato and Itsuki, Kobayashi was tired of fucking around.

Because of Aoki's tragic death, Kobayashi promoted Kenji Yamamoto to Number Three and elevated three of his most trusted and ruthless capos to the management board. Chiharu Toyoda, Kazz Daguchi, and Yuuma Hagihara.

Chiharu Toyoda worked for the Black Rain for fifteen years, specializing in extortion, collection, and arson. Throughout Little Tokyo, dozens of broken bones are attributed to Chiharu, "the *Gorira* (gorilla)" Toyoda. At six feet seven inches and weighing 275 pounds, Chiharu was a formidable force to contend with.

If you missed one payment, you got a warning; if you missed two, he'd break your leg; and if you missed three payments, you were fitted for a pair of cement shoes, and your business would be burnt to the ground.

Kazz Daguchi was the ultimate assassin. Daguchi had a reputation with the yakuza as *yoru no sutōkā* (the night stalker) for his ability to kill his prey without any sign of his being at the scene of the crime. It was rumored that he was so stealthy that he could walk across a room covered with rice paper on the floor, and you would never know he was ever there.

And finally, there is Yuuma Hagihara, a ninja master, and *Kensei* (sword saint), a title given to a warrior of legendary skill in swordsmanship. It is rumored that he can slice a piece of wagyu beef so thin that it has only one side. Hagihara has killed over forty men in samurai duels. He considered himself a *rōnin* (a samurai for hire); he had no master other than himself. Hagihara had been known to switch sides in a battle if he thought it would be advantageous. Hagihara is ruthless, ferocious, and cunning.

Kobayashi looked at his lieutenants and said, "Tell me about this *gaijin*, Baker."

"His name is Butch Baker; he was a pilot during the war. He flew bombers in the Pacific. He was stationed in Yokohama after the war, where he met the whore Aiko. According to Yamato and Itsuki, she's trained in the martial arts. As far as we can tell, they have no relatives living. At least not in Los Angeles." Aoi Yamaguchi, his Number Two, said.

"Tell me about this paint store. What is its layout, and what is the weak point?" Kobayashi asked.

"I am sorry *oyabun*. I do not know?" Yamaguchi answered.

"You mean you haven't been into the store?"

"No, I am ashamed to say," He said.

Kobayashi's anger grew. " Have any of you been to this paint store to see who and what we are dealing with?" he growled at his lieutenants.

They all shook their heads.

"*Orokamono* (idiots)!" He snarled.

An hour later, a well-dressed Japanese man walked into the *Natsukashī Kokoro*. Marlboro and Wakabayashi immediately recognized Kobayashi from his police dossier.

"Good day, sir; how may I help you?" Marlboro asked.

"I am looking to acquire various latex emulsions to cover the interior walls of my abode."

"What colors did you have in mind?" Marlboro asked.

Kobayashi pulled out a piece of paper with names of colors written in Japanese and handed it to Marlboro.

Marlboro looked at the note and called out, "Aiko! Could you come here, please?"

When Wakabayashi came out from the backroom, Kobayashi looked surprised to see what a wisp of a thing this girl who had whipped some of his toughest *Shikkō-sha* (enforcers).

"Yeah, Butch?"

"Can you help me? This gentleman has some paint colors he's interested in," He said as he gave Wakabayashi the note.

She smiled at the leader of the Black Rain and said, "Okay, let's see what we have here. *Tamago-iro* (egg-colored), *Yamabukicha* (gold-brown), *Rokōcha* (contemplation in a tea garden), *Hiwacha* (finch-brown), and *Kariyasu* (Japanese triandra grass)."

"You have?" Kobayashi asked.

"Well, no, but I can have these for you by Friday. Will that be okay?"

"*Hai. Kin'yōbi wa daijōbudeshou* (yes, Friday will be fine)."

"Good. I look forward to seeing you Friday, Mister?"

"Oba. Giichi Oba."

"Mister Oba. *Sayōnara*," Wakabayashi said as she gave a short bow.

Kobayashi returned the gesture and said, "*Sayōnara*."

The District Attorney's office convinced the judge that Riku Usui and Goro Miake were a menace to the Little Tokyo community, and bail was denied. At the same time, Ichiro Hamaguchi and Haruto Sugimoto were being held in the Los Angeles County Jail Infirmary.

It turned out that Riku Usui and Goro Miake were placed in the general population. Unfortunately for them, several WWII veterans who had fought in the Pacific,

Guadalcanal, Saipan, Guam, Wake Island, and Okinawa were also in the general population.

An ex-Marines Gunnery Sergeant named Eduardo Guzman came across Riku Usui and Goro Miake in the yard shortly after they had arrived. Gunny Guzman was serving two life sentences for killing his wife and her lover. He came home unexpectedly after being discharged early from active duty for being wounded and receiving a Purple Heart, Bronze Star, and the Navy Cross for his actions in the taking of Okinawa.

When he found his wife and lover in bed, Guzman removed the .45 revolver from his duffel bag and proceeded to empty the eight-round clip into the copulating couple while he screamed, "Oorah!"

He was tried in civil court since he had been discharged from the Marines only weeks earlier. Although the judge was considering his gallant service and war record when his wife's mother started in on him for killing her daughter, Guzman jumped over the railing and began to strangle her; the judge sentenced him to life in prison with no chance of parole.

Figuring he had nothing to lose, Guzman became the meanest son of a bitch in the joint. He was constantly getting into fights with not only inmates but with the guards as well. He spent most of his time in the 'Hole.'

The Gunny had just been released from six weeks in solitary confinement for smashing a fellow inmate's head in with a ten-pound barbell, cracking his head open, and sending the prisoner into the infirmary, where he is still cooperating.

When Guzman saw Usui and Miake in the yard, he rushed up to the two yakuza and yelled, "Hey, Tojo! What the fuck do you think you're doing?"

"We are doing nothing," Miake replied.

"You two slant-eyes are not allowed in my yard. If I see either one of you in my yard again, I'll kill you both. Understand!"

Riku Usui stood defiant and said, "This is not your yard."

By then, seven other ex-WWII vets had gathered around Usui and Miake in a circle. Feeling threatened, Riku struck a karate defensive stance.

"Well, looky here, boys. Tojo wants to dance," Guzman snickered while he pulled out a shiv made with a broken toothbrush and razor blade.

As Riku did a flying roundhouse kick, knocking down one of the vets and breaking his jaw, Gunny Guzman and the other vets rushed in and brought Usui and Miake down to the ground. All the marines pulled shivs and began stabbing and sticking the two Japanese warriors. The entire prison population in the yard bolted over to cheer the vets on.

By the time the guards began dragging bodies off of the writhing, squirming, killing wolf pack, Riku and Goro were nothing more than two hundred pounds of ground Wagyu Beef.

The prison guard up in the tower began firing his Thompson sub-machine gun at the melee, dispersing the throng of yardbirds.

"Everyone lay flat on the ground.! Anyone standing up will be shot!" The tower guard announced over his PA.

All 500 cons dropped onto the ground. Guzman and the other vets were placed in shackles, dragged away, and placed into solitary.

At their trial, Guzman and the other veterans pleaded self-defense. Since Riku and Goro were dead and over twenty convicts swore that the two Japanese prisoners started the altercations, Guzman and his co-defendants were given another two life sentences.

When Guzman was finally released back into the general prison population, he got a standing ovation and chants of "*Banzai*! (hurrah)"

Detective Sergeant Tanaka got the call about the homicide of a known Black Rain capo, Minato Aoki. He arrived just as the M.E. pulled up in the 'meat wagon.'

"Hey, Doc," Tanaka said.

"What do we have, Detective?" Doctor Gyening asked.

"From what I hear, a dead yakuza."

'Murder?"

"Let's go see," Tanaka said with a grin.

The uniformed policeman standing guard at the crime scene was Officer Rusty Shackleford, an LAPD veteran of eighteen years who had been working in Little Tokyo for the past three years. He was a highly decorated officer and well-respected within the force. Shackleford was pushing fifty. He was a large man, at six feet and weighing 210, but he could still run down most perps when needed. Tanaka was glad to have such a man on his team.

"Hey, Detective."

"So, Rusty, what do we have?" Tanaka asked.

"One Minato Aoki, of Japanese descent. The landlord found him, Mrs. Wilson, when she noticed a foul odor emanating from the apartment. When she entered, she found Mr. Aoki sitting on a floor pillow with a small sword sticking out of his stomach."

"And where is Mrs. Wilson now?" Tanaka asked.

"She's at the station house waiting to be interviewed. When I went in, it was a shambles; it looked like a possible robbery."

"Thanks, Rusty," Tanaka said as he and Doctor Gyening entered the apartment.

"Whatta think, Doc? How long has he been sitting here?"

After a cursory examination, Gyening concluded that Aoki had been dead for at least five days.

"I guess there's no question how he was killed."

"It was murder. The angle of the stab wound would rule out suicide. I'll know more once I open him up," Gyening said.

The M.E. turned to the body collection team and said, "Okay, boys, take him away. You'll have my repost in the morning, Detective."

"Thanks, Doc."

Tanaka walked through Aoki's apartment. At first glance, it did appear to be. A robbery gone bad, but Tanaka had seen hundreds of robberies, and this one was staged to look like a burglary.

The latent print team had failed to produce usable fingerprints. When Tanaka spotted the open Johnny Walker Blue Label bottle, he told the crime scene investigators to collect it.

"I want you to note and send me any information you find on the bottle and label," Tanaka said.

"Yes, sir," CSI Davidson answered.

On his way out, Tanaka stopped by Officer Shackleford, "Rusty, after CSI leaves, be sure to seal everything up."

"Will do."

Chapter Nine
Fort Knox

"Mrs. Wilson, I'm Detective Sergeant Tanaka. I want to thank you for coming down to speak with me."

Mrs. Wanda Wilson weighed all of ninety pounds, soaking wet. She looked to be in her late sixties, but she was only forty-eight; chain smoking and excessive drinking will do that to you. Her cigarette of choice was Lucky Strike, which she smoked one right after another, using the last butt to light the next one. Wearing a simple sack dress that hadn't been washed in over a month, she reeked of stale cigarettes and cheap booze.

Fidgeting in her seat, Tanaka could tell she wasn't thrilled to be sitting in a cold, drab interview room for over an hour. Her scowl and off-putting body language telegraphed that she wasn't thrilled to be there.

"Yeah, like I had a choice," She snapped.

"What can you tell me about Mr. Aoki?"

"You got any cigarettes? I'm all out."

"I'm sorry, I don't smoke."

"Well, does anyone in this dump smoke? I ain't talking unless I get a cigarette!" she demanded.

As he headed toward the door, Tanaka said, "I'll see what I can do."

"I only smoke Lucky Strikes!" She hollered at him.

In the squad room, Tanaka asked, "Does anyone here smoke Lucky Strikes?"

"I do," Detective Juneau said.

"Great. Let me have the pack."

"But this is a new pack. I just bought them."

Tanaka reached into his pocket and pulled out a quarter, "Here, treat yourself."

As Tanaka walked away, Juneau humbly said to the others in the squad room, "I just bought them."

Detective Sergeant Tanaka tossed the unopened pack of Lucky's onto the desk in front of the old crone.

"Here you go."

He could see her disposition changed from annoying to agreeable. She relished opening the new pack with such joy, as if it were an exotic gift. As she took a deep breath, inhaling the aroma of fresh tobacco, she smiled and said, "LSMFT. Lucky Strike Means Fine Tobacco. That's their slogan."

She gingerly took a fag out of the pack and lit it with her well-worn Zippo lighter, took a deep drag, and looked orgasmic as she did.

"Now, Mrs. Wilson, What can you tell me about Mr. Aoki?"

"Like what?"

"Do you know if he had any beefs with the other tenants?"

"How would I know? I'm no gossip!"

"Well, you're the landlady. Surely, you would know if anyone complained about him."

"As far as I know, he got along with the others."

"Now, your apartment is right across from Mr. Aoki's apartment, is that correct?"

"That's right."

"Would you know if he had a lot of visitors?"

"No."

"No, what? No, you don't know, or no, he didn't have a lot of visitors."

"No, I don't know if he had a lot of visitors. I'm no busybody! I don't spend all my time watching the comings and goings of every tenant," Mrs. Wilson said, taking a long drag off of her Lucky.

"Look, Mrs. Wilson, you'll get out of here much quicker if you cooperate. I tell you what, why don't you tell me what you do know, all right?"

"Fine! Last Tuesday night, I just happened to see Aoki and another Jap, no offense, going up to Aoki's apartment. The other man was toting a bottle of Johnny Walker Blue Label, and when he left, he must have left the booze behind because he didn't have it with him. He was carrying a rather large picture of what looked to be a large Japanese painting."

"Can you describe this man?" Tanaka asked.

"Like I said, he was a Jap."

"Yes, so you said. But was he tall or short? Fat or thin? What was he wearing, a suit or work clothes? Did he have any facial hair? Was he bald? Would you be able to recognize him if you saw him again?"

Wilson closed her eyes as if she were thinking. When she opened them again, she said, "He was short, pudgy, full head of hair, clean-shaven, and wore round-rimmed glasses and a suit."

"Very good, Mrs. Wilson. I want to show you some photos, and you tell me if you recognize anyone, if that's okay with you."

"Okay. But let's be quick about it. I want to get home and watch *Queen for a Day*; it starts in an hour."

"We'll have you home in plenty of time," Tanaka said reassuringly.

Tanaka laid out eight photographs for a photo lineup; four were known yakuza members of the Black Rain, and four were Japanese police officers.

"That's him!" Wilson said as she pointed to the photograph of Kenji Yamamoto.

Marlboro and Wakabayashi were setting up a window display for a special sale celebrating Little Tokyo's sixty-fifth Anniversary when a Foack f Fordour-door sedan came tearing down First Street. Hanging out of the passenger's front and back seat windows, two men began firing Thompson sub-machine guns at *Natsukashī Kokoro's* storefront picture windows. Marlboro and Wakabayashi would have been food for the worm farm if it hadn't been for the bulletproof windows.

By the time Tanaka showed up, Marlboro and Wakabayashi were standing out on the curb, being interviewed by Police Officer Rusty Shackleford.

"So, Mr. Baker, can you tell me what happened?"

"Aiko, my wife, and I were putting up a window display when suddenly, a black Ford came screaming by with guns a blazing."

"Any idea who it was?" Shackleford asked.

"Sorry, I don't. It happened so fast," Marlboro said.

"Mrs. Baker, is there anything else you might be able to tell me?"

"No, Officer Shackleford. As my husband said, it happened so fast."

Tanaka walked up to Marlboro and Wakabayashi, talking to Shackleford.

"Officer Shackleford, what have you?" He asked.

"It's a drive shooting, sir."

"Any idea whose responsible, Mr. Baker?" Tanaka asked Marlboro.

"Sorry, Detective Tanaka, as I told Officer Shackleford, it happened so fast. All I saw was a black Ford sedan with two guys hanging out of the passenger side with Tommy guns."

"Officer Shackleford, please take the Bakers downtown to the interview room?"

"Of course. Mr. and Mrs. Baker, this way, my car is right here," Shackleford said.

"Let me just lock up the store," Marlboro said.

Once at the police station, Marlboro and Wakabayashi were taken to the same interrogation room Mrs. Wilson had sat in days earlier.

Before Shackleford left them, he asked, "Can I get you folks a coffee?"

"Yes, two, please," Marlboro said.

"How do you take 'em?"

"Mud," Marlboro replied.

"You got it. Be right back."

Officer Shackleford returned with two cups of black coffee a few minutes later.

"Thanks," Marlboro said.

"Here you go," Shackleford said as he placed the coffees in front of them.

Marlboro and Wakabayashi sat quietly, drinking their drinks and waiting for Tanaka to come in.

"John, Officer Wakabayashi. How are you? I want the truth," Tanaka said.

"Honestly, I'm a little shaken up," Wakabayashi admitted.

"I would be surprised if you weren't. And you, Marlboro, how are you?" Tanaka asked.

"Oh, you know me, I've been shot at by the best of them. I am thankful for having the bulletproof glass installed; that was smart thinking on your part."

"Wow, coming from you, that is high praise."

"Well, don't get a swell head just because you have one good idea," Marlboro joked.

"I'll go ahead and have the windows replaced tomorrow. Is there anything else that you need?"

"Yes, I would like a safe room built upstairs in the living room, masquerading as a bookcase. It must be large enough so Wakabayashi and I can sleep inside, and I can rig some trip wires to alert us if and when we get some intruders."

"Is there room to build one so it doesn't look phony?"

"Yeah, I have a sketch I drew that I think will work."

Tanaka took a look and said, "I'll have my guys start on this tomorrow as well."

"Great."

"Wakabayashi, are you sure you want to go with this assignment? There will be no negative consequences if you decide to leave." Tanaka said.

"Thank you, sir. But I want to continue," She said.

"Are you sure?"

"I'm sure."

Kobayashi and his lieutenants were meeting about the failed assault on the paint store.

"What the Hell went wrong? They were standing in the window like two sitting ducks!" Kobayashi howled.

Aoi Yamaguchi, the number two, tried to deflect the blame onto Chiharu Toyoda, the man who drove the car and was carrying out Yamaguchi's plan.

"I devised a fool-proof plan; Toyoda messed up."

"How was I to know they had bullet-proof windows?"

"You should have checked it out!" Yamaguchi yapped.

"Oh, yeah, well, if you…" Toyoda began to reply but was interrupted.

Kobayashi pounded the tabletop to stop the bickering, "Aoi, it was your plan. It was your responsibility to know such things. Next time, do not fail me!"

Sato, the office lackey, slinked into the room and timidly said, "Kobayashi-san, you have a phone call."

"Can't you see we're in a meeting!" Kobayashi snapped.

"A million pardons. It's Tokyo calling. They say it's urgent."

Kobayashi's face turned ashen as he tried to show no sign of fear. He failed. As he got up from the chabudai to take the phone call, a slight smile could be detected on Aoi Yamaguchi's face.

"*Hai*?" Kobayashi said nervously.

It was the voice of God, the supreme leader of the Black Rain Yakuza International, Hiroshi Takahashi. The man who lorded life and death over every one of the 3000 members of the Black Rain.

"Kobayashi, I have heard some bothersome things. Are they true?" Takahashi gnarled.

"No, *masutā* (master)."

"So, the reports of you having troubles with a *gaijin* are false?"

"I will admit he has proven to be sly, but I can assure you that he will be taken care of."

"A sly one? How many men have you lost?"

"Four, *masutā*," Kobayashi said sheepishly.

"Four!" Takahashi screamed.

The phone was silent for several minutes until Takahashi calmly said. "If this problem is not solved soon, I would hate to think that the world would be a better place without Kio Kobayashi around," Takahashi said with a bone-chillin' tone.

"It shall be solved, *oyabun*."

Before he could say goodbye, the phone went ominously dead.

On returning to the conference room, Kobayashi knew who the rat had betrayed him and contacted Takahashi. Aoi Yamaguchi, Number Two, who had been scheming ever since that *gaijin,* came into Little Tokyo to fuck him over so he could become Number One. If that little fucker wanted war, he got just one.

By the time Marlboro and Wakabayashi returned to the paint store, work had already begun to replace the bulletproof picture windows. The front door was changed out with an all-steel electric open door with no door handle and lock, so there could be no visible way to force entry. Work on the safe room was also in progress. The estimated time for completion of the fortified room was ten hours. It would be ready for Marlboro and Wakabayashi to sleep in that evening.

While the workmen were busy, Marlboro and Wakabayashi went to J.C. Penny's to purchase a couple of sleeping bags, some flashlights, and plenty of batteries. They then stopped at Vroman's Bookstore to buy dozens of used books to fill up the bookshelves that hid the safe room door.

When they returned, Detective Tanaka was waiting for them.

"Butch, Aiko, how are you?" He asked.

"We're fine, Detective. Please come in. Can we offer you some coffee?" Marlboro asked.

"Yes, thank you."

The three of them went upstairs to where the builders were finishing the "bookcase." They would have sworn it belonged in the original room if they hadn't known the bookcase was a new addition.

"So, Whatta think?" Tanaka asked.

"Wow!" Wakabayashi said.

"Great job," Marlboro replied.

"I also had them replace all the apartment windows with bullet-proof glass, like the ones downstairs, as well as having put solid steel retractable window security burglar bars set into the concrete in the living room as well as in the bedroom."

"Thank you, Detective Tanaka. I feel better," Wakabayashi said.

"The place feels like Fort Knox," Marlboro added.

"I thought when the shit hits the fan, you should have an edge. God knows you have the firepower."

"I have a couple of tricks of my own that I plan on implementing. A few you-it-yourself fun projects, as it were," Marlboro said with a wolfish grin.

"I don't even want to know," Tanaka said.

When the Detective left, Marlboro removed two landing lights from a Lockheed F-104 Starfighter that a friend procured for him as a favor. He rigged the lights to be directed at the living room windows and devised a tripwire to set them off. He then unlocked the living room window bars and cracked the windows open.

"Why are you opening the windows? Aren't you just inviting trouble?" Wakabayashi asked.

"I hope so."

"Why?"

"I'm trying to thin the herd and even the odds," Marlboro said with a wink.

His next project was to set up a secret peephole in the bookcase so they could observe any interlopers while they were within the safe area. He fitted a working electrical outlet high in one of the bookshelves with only one of the plugs working while the other had an eyelet for viewing. The working outlet had a plug for a low-wattage light attached to the bookcase.

Marlboro then set up several lighted silent alarms to alert them if anyone entered the apartment while they were sleeping in the safe room. He also fixed a pressure plate on the fire escape to signal if someone was climbing the stairs.

Finally, he fabricated a device that enabled the fire escape to detach from the building and collapse into the alley.

"What happens if they set the building on fire?" Wakabayashi asked.

"Not to worry, doll; I have rappelling ropes that we can use," Marlboro said with an ear-to-ear grin.

"Swell."

Chapter Ten
3 Assassins

Kobayashi had his spies follow Yamaguchi for weeks, gathering all the dirt they could find on his nemeses. For the longest time, they found nothing. The *oyabun* was getting frustrated until he got word of Yamaguchi having sex with an underage preteen schoolgirl. He used the same room on the top floor at the Little Tokyo Hotel, room 424. He would pick her up outside the Maryknoll Grade School every Thursday and take her up to the room where he would have anal and oral sex with her; afterward, he would give her ten dollars and a bag of candy, including Tootsie Roll Pops, Root Beer Barrels, Chuckles, and Bit O Honey.

Kobayashi saw his opportunity to bring Yamaguchi down. He had made the owner of the Hotel an offer he couldn't refuse. For the use of room 423 and putting in a two-way mirror that would be able to spy on Yamaguchi's little sexcapade, he would forgo all protection and extortion fees. It was an offer too good to pass up.

Construction began immediately. By the time Yamaguchi brought his "date" the following Thursday, the mirror had been installed over the queen-size bed. When Yamaguchi saw it, he immediately called down to the front desk.

"This is 424; why was this mirror installed?"

"Because of your great patronage, the owners thought it would be a small token of our thanks, Mr. Yamaguchi. We hope you like it," The manager said.

Yamaguchi did, indeed. He quickly got undressed, laid his head at the foot of the bed so he could see, and watched excitedly as little Mizuki performed oral sex. He loved seeing her tiny head bobbing up and down in the mirror. Not as much as Kobayashi, who was standing next to the cameraman filming Yamaguchi's child pornography debut. For the next four Thursdays, Kobayashi not only had motion pictures taken but still photography too.

"Kobayashi-san, I think it's time that we think about getting rid of that *gaijin* scum. I have a couple of assassins that I could call to rub out those fucking paint jockeys once and for all," Yamaguchi said.

"Who are these assassins?" Kobayashi asked.

"I worked with some men when I was in San Francisco. They are very dependable. You can trust me, *oyabun*."

"If you say they're trustworthy, go ahead with your plan. I trust you."

Yamaguchi planned to have three incompetents bungle the job and pin the failure on Kobayashi, hoping the supreme leader, Hiroshi Takahashi, would have Kobayashi terminated with extreme prejudice. But unbeknownst to him, Kobayashi had informed Takahashi that Yamaguchi had sworn that his "torpedoes" were the right men for the job. Takahashi asked why Kobayashi would allow his underling to make such a decision.

"I felt it was time for him to step up and become a leader," Kobayashi explained.

Takahashi knew what Kobayashi was up to, but he was always willing to let these internal struggles play out as long as they didn't interfere with business. Either way, one would become the victor, and the other would perish.

"*Sore ga jinseida* (such is life)," Takahashi would say.

Jiro, Daichi, and Minato were given instructions to kill the *gaijin* Butch Baker and his whore of a wife, Aiko. Afterward, they were to bring Yamaguchi proof of their death by delivering the little finger of their left hand.

Yamaguchi knew that these three were major fuck-ups; they had always been given the most menial crappiest jobs. They were surprised when given this opportunity. Jiro, Daichi, and Minato had been dubbed the nickname as the three stooges.

"Why, honorable Yamaguchi-san, have you chosen we lowly servants to carry out such a distinguished mission?" Jiro asked.

Yamaguchi looked at the three of them and spoke sincerely, "I can honestly say that I believe you are the only man for this job. I have every confidence that you will bring honor to Black Rain."

Jiro, Daichi, and Minato had each been given an untraceable .38 snub-nosed pistol, a stolen car with a fake license plate, and the standard-issue black pants, sweater, and balaclava.

As they drove around the paint store and down the alley, they spotted that the second-story windows were open to combat the heat from the Santa Ana winds.

"Jiro, look an open window; the gods are finally shining upon us," said Daichi.

"Maybe. This *gaijin* Butch Baker is a worthy adversary. He is already responsible for the deaths of four Black Rain yakuza and put two more in the hospital," Jiro replied.

Minato, who usually remains silent, said, "We must prove ourselves worthy even upon our deaths as long as we are victorious."

"We shall return at three a.m. to *korosu* (kill) Butch Baker and his *baishunpu* (whore)!" Jiro said.

As they drove off, the three assassins screamed, "*Banzai! Banzai! Banzai!*"

Jiro, Daichi, and Minato slowly drove down the alley behind the *Natsukashī Kokoro* paint store. As they approached, they cut off the engine half a block away and silently cruised toward their destination. They couldn't believe their luck; the window to the apartment was still open. Before getting out of the car, the three donned their balaclavas and checked their guns.

"Let's go!" Jiro whispered.

Like three rats, they scampered across the alley toward the fire escape. Silently, they brought the fire escape ladder down, and with great stealth, they began to climb up. Unknowingly, they stepped on the pressure plate, tripping the silent alarm and alerting Marlboro that danger was imminent.

"Wakabayashi! Wake up. We have company. Lock the case after I leave, and stay put," Marlboro said as he handed her a Walther PPK pistol.

He took with him the 9mm Parabellum Browning machine pistol and Browning A5 12-gauge shotgun. Marlboro made his way to the other side of the living room wall and waited. He pumped the Browning and slipped a round into the chamber.

Jiro peeked into the dark living room, trying to adjust his eyes to the layout. As time passed, he could begin to make out the layout: a large bookcase off to his right, a couch and coffee table directly in front of him, and a doorway off to his left, presumably the entrance to the bedroom. There appeared to be another doorway in front of him; he guessed it to be the entrance to the paint store below.

As he watched, he could hear the ticking of a wall clock in the distance. It was very soothing, and the rhythmic tick, tick, tick under different circumstances would quickly put him to sleep.

When he felt it was safe to enter, Jiro climbed into the living room and stood still against the window, holding his .38 ready. He signaled for Daichi to climb in when he thought it was safe. Finally, he waved Minato the all-clear to enter the window. The three of them stood silently by the windows, armed and ready. When Jiro thought it safe to go, he took the lead and began to enter the living room. When he tripped the wire, he had gotten no more than fifteen feet with his compadres by his side, triggering the switch that illuminated the two Lockheed F-104 Starfighter landing lights. The blinding lights were so bright; it was as if they were staring into the sun and almost as hot; they felt as if their faces were melting. Their reaction was naturally to cover their faces. That's when Marlboro, wearing welder's glasses, swung around the doorway and opened fire with the Browning A5 12-gauge shotgun, killing the three stooges quicker than you could say, "Moe, Larry, Curly, or Shemp."

BLAM! BLAM! BLAM!

The air in the apartment was filled with gun smoke and the smell of gunpowder as Jiro, Daichi, and Minato lay dead or dying, their gats clutched in their hands. Marlboro slowly approached the three bodies, expecting any sudden moves from a possible wounded victim. It's well known in the animal world that a wounded animal is the most dangerous. But when he inspected the intruders, they were, in fact, dead.

Parked at the opposite end of the alley, sitting in the backseat of a black Lincoln Continental, was Kio Kobayashi sipping a cup of sake, patently observing the antics of the three stooges. He watched as they ran across the alley to the fire escape and gingerly ascended the stairs to the open window. He observed them waiting until the leader felt safe entering the apartment. It was just seconds when a bright light nearly blinded him. He was reminded of the flash of light he had experienced at Hiroshima as a young lieutenant in the Emperor's 2nd Army. The only reason he survived the bombing was that most of the reinforced concrete buildings on the base were of far stronger construction because of the danger of earthquakes in Japan. This robust construction accounted for the fact that the framework of the buildings he was working in at the time did not collapse.

He ended up spending several months in the hospital with radiation burns on his back and legs; he was luckier than most of the 145,000 people who perished that August 6th.

Nanoseconds after the intense burst of light came three shotgun blasts, then silence and a return to darkness.

Kobayashi tapped his driver on the shoulder and said, "*Sāikō* (let's go)."

As they were leaving the alley, Kobayashi could hear the sound of approaching police car sirens. He smiled, knowing it would be Yamaguchi's head on the chopping block, not his.

"*Sore ga jinseida* (such is life)," Kobayashi whispered.

Hana Wakabayashi saw the lights from the F-104 Starfighter peeking through the bookcase's seams, then heard three shotgun blasts, then darkness and silence.

"Aiko. It's safe to come out now," Marlboro said as he turned on the overhead light in the living room.

She emerged from the safe room to find three lifeless bodies of men dressed all in black. As many times as she had seen death, she'd never quite gotten used to it. The blood and carnage. The almost dance-like poses of the spiritless as they lie in their blood and bodily fluids with that grey pallor and wanes in their eyes.

"Did you have to kill them?" She asked.

"Yes, I did. What did you think they were coming over for a bit of sukiyaki? See those Roscoes that they are holding in their hands. They would have killed us both without a second thought. Listen, doll; it's only going to get rougher, not easier. I need to know right now if I can count on you. Are you in or out?" Marlboro asked.

"I'm in," Wakabayashi said.

Detective Tanaka, Detective Juneau, and Detective Bell, along with four black-and-whites and the Medical Examiner showed up with flashing lights in front of the *Natsukashī Kokoro* paint store.

"This is becoming a habit, Mr. Baker," Tanaka said.

"Tell me about it. It's getting so one can't fall asleep without some asshole climbing in the window with a gat in his hand," Marlboro said.

"Maybe you should try keeping the windows locked," Detective Juneau said.

"Yeah, you try sleeping in this cracker box with the windows closed. It's like an oven in here with the windows closed. This place ain't got no air conditioning. Whatta think this is the Ritz?" Marlboro said.

"Why didn't you lock the solid steel retractable window security burglar bars, Mr. Baker?" Detective Bell asked.

"Geez, I must have forgot. I thought I did. Oops, my mistake. Thanks for pointing that out, Detective Bell. I'll be sure to do that right now," Marlboro said as he walked over to the living room windows and locked the security bars.

Tanaka approached the Medical Examiner, Doctor Gyening, and asked, "So, Doc, what do you have?"

"Yup, it's pretty straightforward. All three died from a single wound from a shotgun blast. No identification on any of them," Doctor Gyening answered.

"Thanks, Doc."

"Can I take the bodies away, now?" Gyening asked.

"Yeah, get them out of here," Tanaka said.

As they were carrying the bodies of Jiro, Daichi, and Minato out on stretchers, Tanaka asked Marlboro and Officer Wakabayashi, "Have either of you seen any of these men before?"

"No," Wakabayashi said.

"Never laid eyes on any of them," Marlboro added.

"Okay, everybody, let's wrap this up; it's late," Tanaka said, ushering everyone out.

Once everyone had left, Tanaka barked, "Just what the Hell were you thinking, Marlboro!"

"This is war, Detective. There aren't any rules in a street fight. It's kill or be killed, and if it's all the same with you, I'd rather be the one killing and not the one getting killed. So, I'm just evening out the opposition," Marlboro snapped back.

"Okay, okay. It's just that I'm starting to get heat from above. I'm sorry."

"Look, Yuki, I get it if you want to pull the plug on this. But I think things are moving in the right direction. If they continue taking heavy casualties, they will either have to fish or cut bait," Marlboro said.

"And you think you and Wakabayashi are up for the task?"

Marlboro looked over at Wakabayashi and said, "I trust this doll with my life."

Kobayashi and two of his goons knocked on the plate glass window to get Wakabayashi's attention since the front door had been replaced with a solid metal electronic activated door. Wakabayashi shouted out to Marlboro, "Butch, Mr. Kobayashi is here."

Marlboro tucked his Walther PPK pistol into the waistband of his pants and untucked his shirt. As he appeared from the back of the store, he shouted, "Okay, Aiko, let them in."

Wakabayashi hit the buzzer, and the front door sprung open. The three men entered the store, all impeccably dressed in tailor-made sharkskin suits.

"*Ohayōgozaimasu*, Kobayashi-san (good morning, Mr. Kobayashi)," Wakabayashi said with a bow.

"*Ohayōgo*," Kobayashi said as he returned the bow.

"Are you here for your paint?" Marlboro asked.

"*Hai.*"

"Great. I have them right here behind the counter," Marlboro said as he led the group to the counter where the cash register was located. Under the counter sat a loaded Browning Automatic Rifle, just in case.

Marlboro pulled five one-gallon paint cans from under the counter. Wakabayashi rang up the total on the register:

"That's five gallons at fifteen dollars each. It's seventy-five dollars."

As Kobayashi reached for his wallet, Marlboro read off the paint titles: "Let see, we have *Tamago-iro* (egg-colored), *Yamabukicha* (gold-brown), *Hiwacha* (finch-brown), *Rokōcha* (contemplation in a tea garden), and *Kariyasu* (Japanese triandra grass)."

Kobayashi counted out seventy-five dollars, handed the cash to Wakabayashi, and nodded to his thugs that they should pick up the paint cans.

"*Soto de mate* (wait outside)," He ordered.

They did as they were told.

"*Arigatō* (thank you)," Marlboro said with a bow.

Kobayashi gave a guttural grunt and a smile. Then he asked. "What was all the commotion last night? I heard someone broke into your apartment," He said.

"Yeah, that's the second time this has happened," Marlboro said.

"Anybody hurt?"

"Three Jap Hatchet men died from a little Chicago lightning. No offense."

"Chicago lightning?"

"Yeah, you know, gunfire. I shot and killed all three. It was like when we stormed Okinawa. I musta killed a couple of dozen of them Japs that day. No offense," Marlboro said with a hint of bravado to see if he could get a rise from Kobayashi.

The inscrutable *oyabun* looked poker-faced, not showing any reaction at all.

"Yeah, this is the second time some Jap goombahs tried to break in, and the second time they came hauled out of here in a body bag, ya dig?"

"I understand, yes."

"Have you had any trouble with break-ins where you live, Kobayashi-san?"

"No. We have been fortunate."

"What kind of business are you in, Kobayashi-san, if you don't mind my asking?" Marlboro asked.

"I am an entrepreneur. I import and export, do some financing, and provide private security services."

"Was you in the war?" Marlboro asked.

Wakabayashi interrupted, "Butch, honey, don't be talking about such things with our customers. I'm sorry Kobayashi-san."

"You're right, Aiko. Please forgive me, Kobayashi-san," Marlboro apologized.

"No, that is quite all right. Your husband, Mr. Butch, is very courageous. To answer your question, yes, I was in the war. I was stationed at Hiroshima."

"So, you were there when we dropped Little Boy?"

"*Hai*."

Marlboro decided to try to get a rise out of Kobayashi, "Whoo – wee. You must be one tough sumbitch to survive fourteen thousand degrees Fahrenheit. How'd you do it?"

"Butch! Stop it. Please forgive my Butch; he doesn't mean no disrespect. Do you Butch?" Wakabayashi said.

"That's right. Please forgive me, Kobayashi-san," Marlboro apologized again, giving Kobayashi a deep bow.

Kobayashi returned the bow and left the shop, returning to his bodyguards. He got into the backseat of his black Lincoln Continental and drove off.

"Was that really necessary?" Wakabayashi asked.

"What?"

"Provoking Kobayashi that way."

"What better way to get things going than kicking the bear?"

"That's a good way to get eaten!"

"Well, someone once said, sometimes you eat the bear, and sometimes the bear eats you," Marlboro said with a devilish grin.

"My point exactly."

"Well, I, for one, am in the mood for bear stew."

"You're impossible!"

"Hey, doll, what say we go upstairs, get naked, and practice the Dewey Decimal system on each other?"

Aoi Yamaguchi, Little Tokyo's Number Two, sat waiting on the phone for Hiroshi Takahashi - the supreme leader of the Black Rain Yakuza International, to answer.

An anonymous voice said, "Who is calling?"

"Aoi Yamaguchi."

"What is this regarding?"

"I must speak with Takahashi-san. It is urgent!"

"One moment."

"Takahashi-san does not wish to speak to you, sayōnara."

CLICK.

Yamaguchi quickly redialed the number; when the call was answered, the anonymous voice said, "Who is calling?"

"It is Aoi Yamaguchi. I must speak with Takahashi-san."

The anonymous voice said nothing. He just hung up.

CLICK.

Yamaguchi panicked; why wouldn't the supreme leader take his call? He always took his calls. Kobayashi! He must have spoken to Takahashi earlier, that fucking bastard, and laid the blame on those bumbling stooges' failure on him, even though Kobayashi approved the plan and the assassins. He must be removed; he'll enlist Chiharu Toyoda, Kazz Daguchi, and Yuuma Hagihara to dethrone Kobayashi.

He found all three of his potential coup members hanging out at the *Kame* (turtle) Restaurant, having lunch and consuming large quantities of sake.

"I thought I'd find you all here," Yamaguchi said.

"Yamaguchi-san, you don't look too good. What's wrong?" Chiharu Toyoda asked.

"I need your help. It's Kobayashi; he's out of control, making irrational and dangerous decisions. I think it's time to take him out. Can I count on you all to back me up?"

Yuuma Hagihara snickered, "I think it's you that's out of control, Yamaguchi-san."

Yamaguchi was taken aback, "What do you mean?

"Wasn't it you that brought in Jiro, Daichi, and Minato?" Hagihara asked.

"Yes, but…"

"And wasn't it your plan to have them try and enter the Baker's apartment even though Haruto and Riku tried the same thing and failed?"

"Yes, but…"

"We were told that if we see you, we should tell you that *Oyabun* Kobayashi wants to see you right away at his home," Kazz Daguchi said.

"So, you won't help me?" Yamaguchi asked.

"No," Hagihara answered.

Yamaguchi felt walls closing in on him; he had underestimated Kobayashi, and now he was to pay the ultimate consequence for his sloppiness. He pulled his Lincoln Town Car up to Kobayashi's driveway gate and waited for the armed guard to approach.

"Kon'nichiwa, Sato."

"Kon'nichiwa, Yamaguchi-san," The guard said with a slight bow of respect.

Sato gave the inside armed guard the okay signal to open the gate.

Yamaguchi drove the Lincoln up the driveway leading to the house. Once parked, he got out of the car and went to the front door, where he was greeted by two bodyguards who patted him down for any concealed weapons. They found none. They then escorted him to the backyard, where Kobayashi greeted him.

"Yamaguchi-san, the time has come for you to honor the *Bushidō* Code (the way of the warrior) and commit *seppuku* (cutting the belly)."

"I have no intention of committing suicide by *seppuku* or by any other means, and there's nothing you can do or say to make me," Yamaguchi said.

"Really? Take a look at this."

Kobayashi gave Yamaguchi an envelope with a dozen photographs of him engaging in sex with the elementary school girl, Mizuki. Yamaguchi's face turned white, and he began to sweat profusely.

"I also have several hours of motion picture films. I'm sure you and your family would endure much shame and embarrassment if these were to make their way public." Kobayashi said with a slight hint of pleasure.

"Rokudenashi (bastard)."

"You are right. I cannot make you commit *seppuku*, but I am offering you an honorable way out."

"And how do I know you will not release these after I die?"

"You have my word on the *Bushidō* Code."

Yamaguchi resigned himself to his fate, "*Wakatta* (okay). You win."

Kobayashi signaled to his bodyguards to bring out the necessary ceremonial accouterment. As his men set up the traditional mat where Yamaguchi would kneel and the *sanbo* (a small wooden stand where the *tantō* would be placed), Yamaguchi bathed in cold water to prevent excessive bleeding. He was given a white kimono and was served his favorite foods for his last meal.

When he had finished, the knife and cloth were handed to Yamaguchi as he knelt on the mat. Standing directly behind him was the master swordsman, Yuuma Hagihara, who acted as the *kaishakunin* (care worker) and was appointed to behead the one performing *seppuku*.

Chapter Eleven
Seppuku

Yamaguchi was given the opportunity to write his death poem. He could not conceive a proper poem, so he wrote one of his favorite Japanese monks, Shiaku Sho'on.

The Sharp-edged sword, unsheathed,
cuts through the void.
Within the raging fire
a calm wind blows.

Yamaguchi, not wanting to give Kobayashi the pleasure of seeing any weakness in his death, stared Kobayashi in the eye as he opened his kimono, took up the *tanto*, held the blade with the cloth around it, and plunged the blade into his abdomen, making a left-to-right cut. Yuuma Hagihara, the *kaishakunin,* quickly and skillfully performed a *dakikubi* (embraced head) in which a slight band of flesh is left, attaching the head to the body so that the head can dangle in front as if embraced.

As much as Kobayashi detested his opponent, he was impressed at Yamaguchi's *seppuku*. He would report to the supreme leader, Hiroshi Takahashi, that Yamaguchi died the way of the *Bushidō* Code.

Two weeks after his death, an anonymous package was delivered to Wakana Yamaguchi, his widow, containing several dozen photographs and six rolls of motion picture film showing her husband in various acts of sexual deviant behavior with the preteen Mizuki. Shortly after receiving the package,

Wakana Yamaguchi slit her wrists and was found dead in the bathtub by their eldest son, Daiki.

Detective Tanaka and the Homicide Squad received an anonymous tip that a partially decapitated body was in a dumpster behind the *Natsukashī Kokoro* paint store.

After getting the tip, Tanaka called Marlboro and asked him to go into the alley and check to see if there was indeed a body in the dumpster.

"Yuki, it's Marlboro."

"Yeah?"

"You Homicide boys better come on over."

"So, there is a body in the dumpster?"

"Yup. And from what I can tell, it looks like a traditional *hara-kiri* job; he's dressed in a white kimono, his stomach has been slit, and his head is hanging on by a thread."

"We'll be right over. Do me a favor, and don't let anybody mess with the body."

"Roger that."

The first to arrive at the scene was Police Officer Rusty Shackleford, which surprised Marlboro. He knew that it was unusual for a beat cop to arrive before the suits showed up. Something didn't seem kosher with this Shackleford.

"Whatta got?" Shackleford asked.

"I found a body in the dumpster while I was throwing some garbage away."

"Did you call it in?"

"Yeah. A Detective Tanaka said he's on his way."

"Well, you can go. I'll take over from here."

" Detective Tanaka said I should stick around."

"Beat it," Shackleford ordered.

"I'm staying."

Shackleford took out his billy club and began to step toward Marlboro when Tanaka and his crew showed up.

"Shackleford! What's going on?"

"This civilian was interfering with a crime scene."

"This is Mr. Baker, the civilian who called this in. I asked him to stay by the dumpster to keep the lookie-loos from tampering with the crime scene."

"Sorry, sir, I didn't know," Shackleford said apologetically.

"Go out and let the M.E. know where we're at," Tanaka ordered.

"Yes, sir," Shackleford replied as he left the alley.

Tanaka looked at his squad and said, "Okay, gents. Let's start the canvassing and see if anybody saw or knows anything about this."

Once alone, Tanaka asked Marlboro, "Ever seen this guy?"

"No, should I?"

"He was Aoi Yamaguchi. The Number Two in the Black Rain."

"He must have pissed off somebody big time," Marlboro said.

"They could have just whacked him, but they let him die with dignity."

"If that's dignity, just pop a .45 slug in my brain and call it a day."

"In the yakuza samurai code, dying by *seppuku* is an honorable death. So even though he fucked up, he was allowed to die the way of the *Bushidō* Code."

"Gee, that's swell. By the way that, Shackleford's a real goon," Marlboro said.

"Yeah, we've had some complaints about him over the years. But he hasn't fucked up enough to get him kicked him off the force."

"Well, when he does, maybe you can show him the *Bushidō* Code," Marlboro said.

Doctor Gyening, the M.E., took one look at the body in the dumpster and said to his assistants, "Be careful, boys; I want you to get the body with the head still attached."

"It ain't going to be easy, Doc. The head is hanging on by the thinnest layer of epidermis."

"Oh, I know, I can see that. Just do your best."

The two assistants, standing waist-deep in blood and guts, worked gingerly on bringing out what little of Aoi Yamaguchi there was. They were successful in bringing out the head and body intact and being able to carry Yamaguchi out on a stretcher.

"*Seppuku*?" Asked Gyening.

"Yeah, I've never seen one done better. Then they go and throw him away like yesterday's trash," Tanaka said.

"Ah, that's a shame."

"When do you think I can get the autopsy report, Doc?"

"I should have it for you by five o'clock."

"Thanks, Doc."

Once everyone had left the crime scene, Detective Tanaka, Wakabayashi, and Marlboro strolled down the alley.

"Why do you think they dumped the body in our backyard?" Marlboro asked.

"I sense they're sending you a message," Tanaka answered.

"And that would be?"

"*Iku ka shinu ka* (go or die)," Wakabayashi said.

"Jeeze, they could've just sent a note," Marlboro quipped.

"These boys have never been subtle. They like to make a noise," Tanaka said.

"That makes two of us," Marlboro responded.

The footsteps of someone running came from behind them. They turned to see a man welding a *Tachi* saber, holding the sword above his head. He rushed at them, screaming, "*Kōtei banzai* (long live the Emperor)!"

He was upon them so fast that Tanaka nor Marlboro had time to pull their weapons. Wakabayashi calmly took a karate stance, and while his arms were raised above his head, she swiftly swung a sidekick to the man's jaw. The assailant dropped unconscious to the ground like a sack of spuds, suffering a broken jaw.

Marlboro and Tanaka stood in awe of the quick-thinking Wakabayashi. The detective knelt and placed the would-be assassin in handcuffs while calling in for assistance for a black & white to come and haul his ass to the county jail hospital.

"I must say, Officer Wakabayashi, that was a fine display of quick thinking," Tanaka said.

"That's my partner for ya. She's one tough *Shiori Koibito* (white lover), or should I say cookie," Marlboro chuckled.

"Have either one of you seen him before?"

"I haven't. Have you?" Marlboro asked Wakabayashi.

"Never," She said, shaking her head.

The first officer on the scene was Police Officer Rusty Shackleford.

"Well. Well. What do we have here?" Shackleford asked, seeing the perp sprawled on the pavement, unconscious, with Detective Tanaka holding the *Tachi* saber.

"Officer Shackleford, would you be so kind as to take this *tawagoto no ichibu* (piece of shit) and deposit it at the county jail hospital. I'll be along shortly to complete the paperwork," Tanaka said.

"Man, you really kicked ass, sir."

"Oh, it wasn't me. It was Mrs. Baker who put his lights out."

"No, shit! Excuse my French; I mean, no kidding!"

"That's right. You do not want to mess with this lady."

"No, sir! All right, you, get off your dying ass and on your dying feet," Shackleford said as he grabbed the assailant's arm, lifting him onto his feet.

"You want I should take that sword with me as evidence, sir?" Shackleford asked.

"That's okay. I'll bring it down to the station," Tanaka said.

"Very good," Shackleford replied as he led the prisoner to his squad car.

"I'll need you and Mrs. Baker to come down to headquarters and fill out a police report," Tanaka said.

"Let's do it."

Chapter Twelve
Officer Shackleford

"Kobayashi-san, there is a Police Officer Rusty Shackleford requesting an audience with you," said Arata, one of Kobayashi's lackeys.

"I shall see him."

Shackleford entered Kobayashi's private office. Seated behind a large, raised oak desk with two chairs opposite him on a lower level, giving Kobayashi the physiological advantage.

The police officer went to sit down when Kobayashi grunted, "*Oi* (hey)! I did not say you could sit down."

"Sorry." Shackleford apologized.

"What is it you want?"

"I have come with news of the latest attempt on Baker."

"Speak."

"It failed. Baker's wife foiled that attack by knocking your man unconscious and breaking his jaw."

"*Kuso ttare* (God damnit)!" Kobayashi yelled out, slamming his fist on the desk.

Arata came running in, pistol in hand, "*Oyabun*, is everything all right?"

Kobayashi waved Arata away, "Go."

"Officer Shackleford, why did you come here?"

"I thought that you could use some assistance in eliminating Butch Baker," Shackleford said.

"And why would you want to help?"

"Money."

"Ah, money. Yes, of course, please have a seat. What do you propose, Officer Shackleford?"

"I will be your inside man for a nominal monthly fee."

"How nominal?"

"A thousand dollars a month," Shackleford said.

"A thousand dollars a month is a lot of money, Officer Shackleford. I ask for a lot in return for that kind of money."

"Ask, and you shall receive. You won't be sorry."

"If you fail me, it will be you that will be sorry, Officer Shackleford," Kobayashi warned.

At two thirty in the morning, there was a pounding on Kenji Yamamoto's apartment door. Kenji's wife, Chie, jumped up and elbowed her husband, screaming, *"Jishin* (earthquake)!"

Kenji jumped out of bed naked and ran over to pick up his underwear lying on the floor. As he was fumbling to put on his boxer shorts, another pounding on the door came, followed by "Police, open up!"

"Get dressed!" Kenji snapped to Chie.

When Kenji opened the door, he was greeted by six uniformed officers and Detective Charlie Bell, who was holding a piece of paper.

"Kenji Yamamoto. We have a warrant to search these premises. Please have a seat on the sofa, you too, ma'am."

They did as instructed.

"Is there any other person in the apartment?" Bell asked.

"No," Kenji answered.

The six officers began to ransack the apartment, going through it like six mini-tornados. After an hour and a half, they had collected several boxes of papers and were preparing to leave when Detective Bell spotted an interesting painting on the living room wall.

"My, that's a lovely painting. Isn't that Hiroshi Yoshida's *Fuji from Kawaguchi Lake*?"

"Yes. My good friend Minato Aoki gave that to me," Yamamoto said.

"Really? That's funny; we have an eyewitness claiming that you were seen taking the painting the day Mr. Aoki was murdered. I must ask you to come with us, Mr. Yamamoto," Bell said.

"Can I at least get dressed?

Kobayashi called the San Francisco branch of the Black Hand and asked his counterpart, Hanzō Doumekii if he could send soldiers to take care of a minor annoyance.

"I hear it's more than a minor annoyance. I hear that it's more of a royal pain in the ass," Doumekii said.

"This paint pusher is disrupting my whole enterprise. I'm tired of playing around. What sort of help can you provide?" Kobayashi asked.

"What's in it for me?"

"Well, there's that to discuss."

"I want twenty percent off the top for one year," Doumekii said.

"Twenty perc…are you fucking out of your mind!"

"Kio, since we're friends, I'll just take ten. You can take it or leave it."

"Ten percent for six months."

There was a momentary silence before Doumekii said, "Deal. But I want it in writing by this afternoon."

A dejected Kobayashi said, "*Sore wa okonawa rerudearou* (it shall be done), but I only want the best you have."

"I will have my top ten *senshi* (warriors) leave for Los Angeles tomorrow," Doumekii said.

"Yoi (good)," Kobayashi growled as he hung up the phone.

Unlike Kobayashi, when Doumekii hung up, he had a grin that reached from ear to ear. After savoring his good fortune, Doumekii pulled out the roster of his top *heitai* (soldiers). He wasn't about to give Kobayashi his very best men; he would send him down his junior varsity team, all good men, just not the A-team.

The following day, Doumekii's men headed down to Los Angeles in two Chevrolet Bel-Air sedans, five in each. One car took the I-5, and the other took the Pacific Coast Highway, which would take longer, but Doumekii didn't want to take any chances. He knew that sentiments toward the Japanese still hadn't totally eased because of the war.

As the car heading down PCH was approaching Garrapata Creek Bridge, Shō Sakyramori, the driver realized they needed to stop for gas. When they crossed the bridge, there was a privately owned Texaco station slash diner named the Duke & Slim's Hamburgers and Bar-B-Q Joint.

"You boys go inside and get a table; I'll be in after I pump some gas," Sakyramori said.

The four others entered the dinner, where several tables with what looked to be locals were eating lunch. The jukebox played Patsy Cline's "Crazy," and the chatter was almost deafening. That all changed when people saw the four Japanese patrons enter the diner. Then things got eerily quiet.

Dotty, the waitress, asked, "Table for four?"

"Five," Masao said as he held up five fingers.

"Follow me, please," Dotty said as she walked them to a table in the back. Once they were seated, she handed them menus.

"I'll be back to take your orders in a minute," she said, going up to the cash register as Shō had come in to pay for the gas.

"That will be Three dollars and sixty cents."

Shō paid for the gas and went to join the others in the back of the restaurant. As he passed one of the tables, a grizzly old fisherman named Tommy 'Two Thumbs' shouted, "Hey, Dot, when did Duke & Slim start serving sukiyaki burgers?"

Masao and the others started to stand when Shō gestured for them to sit back down.

"Just stay calm. We don't need any trouble with these *gesu yarō* (assholes). We'll just eat and leave," Shō said.

Dotty returned to their table and asked, "What can I get you fellas."

The order included four cheeseburgers, one Bar-B-Q pork sandwich, six French fries, and five Coca-Colas.

Sitting with Tommy 'Two Thumbs' Remer was an ex-Navy man, 'Slamming Sammy' Tanner, who was one of the survivors of the attack on Pearl Harbor. When Dotty was bringing back their Cokes, he shouted, "Hey, Tojo, wouldn't you prefer the Jap drink *Ramune* rather than Coca-Cola?"

Masao stood up and yelled, "Listen, old man, you better keep your yap shut before I come over there and shut it for you!"

Sammy jumped up and hollered, "Come on, slant-eye, show me what you got. We kick your fucking ass all across the Pacific, and we're ready to do it again!"

Masao reached behind his back, unsheathed a *tanto*, and sneered, "*Shinu toki ga kita yo, rōjin* (time to die, old man)."

Sammy began to laugh. "Well, Jesus palomino, ain't that just like you sniveling little Jap bastards to bring a knife to a gunfight." He said as he reached behind his back and pulled his G.I.-issued Colt .45.

Shō grabbed Masao's arm and growled, "*Sore o shimatte kudasai* (put that away)!"

He rose from the table, his hands held high as if surrendering. "Look, we don't mean any disrespect. We just want to eat in peace and then leave."

"That ship has sailed, my little yella friend," Tanner said still pointing his pistol at the Masao.

Duke, the café owner, chief cook, and bottle washer, came out from the back after Dotty reported what was happening.

"Sammy, you and Tommy just take a big step back and put that gun away. I don't need no more dead Japs in my diner. You hear!"

The fact that the cook used the phrase "I don't need no more dead Japs" got the entire table's attention. Shō, arms still raised above his head, said, "How about we get those burgers to go?"

Duke agreed. "That sounds like a good idea. I'll have them ready to go in about five minutes. Now, Sammy, you and Tommy just stay cool; you dig!" He said.

"Sorry, Duke, that ship has sailed," Tommy said as he pulled out a Colt – Police .38 Special and pointed it at the gaggle of yakuza soldiers.

"You boys feeling a little kamikaze?" Sammy mocked.

Duke simultaneously pushed Dotty down behind the cash register counter and grabbed his Remington twelve-gauge sawed-off shotgun. From that moment forward, everything began to move in slow motion.

When Masao saw that the other white man, Tommy, pulled a gun, he dropped the *tanto* and took out his Smith and Wesson snub-nose revolver. The three other Black Rain members stood up, holding their pistols, pointing at Sammy and Tommy.

The dozen or so other patrons quickly skedaddled out the front and back doors and ran to their parked cars. Dotty maneuvered her way to the payphone in the hall leading to the bathrooms and called Sheriff Dooley of Monterey County.

"Sheriff Dooley, this is Dotty Steelmen down at Duke & Slim's Hamburgers and Bar-B-Q. We got us a situation here. It looks like Tommy 'Two Thumbs' Remer and 'Slamming Sammy' Tanner are going to shoot it out with a bunch of Japanese. You better get down here ASAP!"

Shō glanced at Masao and the others, smiled, nodded, and reached for his gat; that's when Sammy fired the first shot, hitting Masao in the neck, severing his carotid artery, spraying blood in the faces of his compatriots, temporarily blinding them, allowing Tommy and Sammy the advantage.

BAM.

Shō screamed, "*Banzai*! Die Yankee dog!" as he fired wildly. Still, he was able to hit Tommy 'Two Thumbs' in his hand and left shoulder.

BAM. BAM. BAM. BAM. BAM. BAM.

As a veteran of several battles, Sammy had nerves of steel and carefully aimed as he fired, easily hitting each of the three blood-soaked yakuza. One by one, he skillfully blew large chucks of their skulls off, spraying blood and brains all over the walls behind them as if he were at the duck shooting gallery in the Monterey Carnival penny arcade.

BAM. BAM. BAM.

Within seconds, only Shō was standing; unfortunately, his .38 Smith and Wesson was empty. As he frantically tried to reload, 'Slamming Sammy,' Tanner took aim and fired, striking Shō right between the eye, "Eat lead, Tojo. That's for the boys on the Arizona," Sammy jeered.

BAM.

Duke was amazed at how quickly it was over; he didn't even get a chance to use the sawed-off. Tommy 'Two Thumbs' sat down once the shooting was over as Dotty ran over to apply pressure onto his wounded shoulder.

"Duke, call an ambulance! I already called Sheriff Dooley," Dotty hollered.

With sirens blaring, Sheriff Dooley and Deputy Wiggin's squad cars came to a screeching halt in front of Duke & Slim's Hamburgers and Bar-B-Q Joint, their guns drawn.

"You cover the back!" Dooley shouted as he slowly entered the diner.

Duke met the Sheriff as he came crouching into the beanery. "Sheriff, it's all over," Duke said.

"Jesus H. Christ! This place looks like the storming of Guadalcanal Beach. What the Hell happened, Duke?"

Sammy stepped in and said, "That there Jap pulled a sword on Tommy and me. After I pulled my gun, the rest of them pulled out their roscoes. That's when the shit hit the fan."

"Is that what happened, Dotty?" Dooley asked.

"That's right, Sheriff," she said, leaving out the part where Sammy had started it by insulting the five Japanese patrons.

The ambulance and the medical examiner showed up within the hour. The ambulance arrived to patch up Tommy 'Two Thumbs' Remer, and the M.E. was there to cart off five dead Japanese Americans to the morgue.

"Tommy, I got some good news, and I've got some bad news. The good news is that you're going to live. The bad news is that I don't think anyone will call you Tommy 'Two Thumbs' anymore; your left thumb has been blown clean off. You're going to have to get a new nickname," Roger Cartwright, the ambulance attendant, said with a grin.

"Officer Shackleford, here."

The voice on the other end of the phone was Kenji Yamamoto, "Listen, I just got out on bail. We need to meet."

"What's this about?"

"Kio Kobayashi said that I should call you. That you'll be able to help me."

"Meet me in the parking lot of Tail O the Pup tonight at nine o'clock. I'll be wearing a Brooklyn Dodgers ball cap. Come alone."

CLICK.

At precisely nine o'clock, Yamamoto approached the counter and ordered two hot dogs and a soda. He paid the 25 cents and took his order to Shackleford, who sat nearby.

"Officer Shackleford?"

"Yeah. You Yamamoto?"

"*Hai.*"

"What can I do you for?"

"I've been arrested for murder."

"Gee, that's tough," Shackleford said sarcastically.

"I need your help."

"It'll cost ya."

"How much?"

"Five Gs"

"Five thousand dollars!"

"What's your life worth? You go to the big house, and you are either going to wind up somebody's bitch or wind up dead. It's your call," Shackleford said as he started to get up.

"No. No. Sit down. Okay, five thousand, but it will take me a couple of days to get that kind of money."

"Okay, so you did you kill?"

"I'm accused of killing…"

Shackleford held up his hand, "Look, I don't need the whole song and dance; just give me the name of the stiff."

"Minato Aoki."

"Hmm, I know that name. So, you're the guy who bumped him off with that Jap shiv," Shackleford said.

"Uh, yeah. The cops said that they have a witness."

"So."

"So, I want you to get me the witness's name."

"Then what? You're going to have him whacked? On second thought, I don't want to know," Shackleford said.

"Will you do it?"

"When I get the 5Gs, you get the name."

"I'll have it for you in two days."

"Okay, meet me here Thursday, same time. Now beat it; you're disrupting my digestion."

Kobayashi got word from Hanzō Doumekii in San Francisco, alerting him that half of the men that he sent down had been killed in a shootout near Carmel at some cheesy dincr on the coast.

"Those were five of my best men," Doumekii lied.

"When can I expect replacements?"

"When you send me money."

"For what?"

"For the men that I lost," Doumekii said.

"Exactly. They were your men; when they get here, they're my men. You want a percentage of my territory. You better send me down five men who aren't stupid enough to get rubbed out in some nickel-and-dime diner!" Kobayashi barked and slammed the phone down.

"Her name is Wanda Wilson; she's the landlady at the Harbor Cove Apartments, where you butchered Minato Aoki," Shackleford said.

Yamamoto handed Shackleford a brown envelope containing five thousand dollars.

"It's all there," Yamamoto said.

"It better be. Now scram!"

As Yamamoto walked away, he uttered, "*Buta* (pig)."

"What did you call me?" Shackleford asked, walking right behind Yamamoto.

"What? I didn't say anything," Yamamoto said.

Shackleford gave Yamamoto a hard punch in the kidneys, forcing Yamamoto down to the ground, "You ever call me a pig again, and I'll break your back. Got it, *buta*?"

When Yamamoto returned home, the side where that fucker Shackleford had hit him still hurt, so he took several aspirins. Two hours later, it wasn't feeling any better, and worse yet, when he peed, he peed blood.

"I think you should go see a doctor," Chie, his wife, said.

"No, It will alright."

"Well, if you're still pissing blood in the morning, you're going to the doctor!"

Yamamoto drank two quarts of water before going to bed. He got up four times during the night, and each time he urinated, the amount of blood was less than the previous time.

By eight o'clock, there was hardly any trace of blood, and his side was feeling better.

The phone rang while he was enjoying his traditional Japanese breakfast, consisting of steamed rice, miso soup, grilled fish, pickles, fermented soybeans, seaweed, and tofu.

"It's for you. It's Kobayashi-san," Chie whispered.

"*Moshi moshi* (hello), Kobayashi-san, I got the witness's name. I hoped we could have Chiharu Toyoda take care of the problem."

"No, I think it best that you handle it yourself since you were careless enough to be spotted," Kobayashi said.

"Of course, *oyabun. Sayonara.*"

CLICK.

"What did he say?" Chie asked.

"He said that I have to take care of the old lady myself."

"So, getting rid of an old woman shouldn't be too hard. You take care of her, and when you return, I'll make your favorite dish, *shirako* (fish prostate)."

"And *torisashi* (raw chicken)?" He pleaded.

"Sure, baby. But you got to go and kill the old bitch first. Now go and make me proud."

Chapter Thirteen
Wanda Wilson

Wanda Wilson was enjoying her third cup of Maxwell House Original Roast and sixth Lucky Strike cigarette as she watched her favorite morning TV show, Queen for a Day, on her sofa in her tattered quilted housecoat.

She was so engrossed in Jack Baily preparing to announce the woman about to be crowned Queen for a Day that she didn't hear the kitchen back door being jimmied open. Kenji Yamamoto slipped into the kitchen and withdrew a large butcher's knife from the knife block. He carefully peeked around the doorway that led into the living room where Wanda was sitting. Holding the knife to slit her throat, he moved silently toward her, inch by inch.

The old landlady seemed glued to the TV, oblivious to the assassin standing within striking distance. She held her seventh Lucky Strike in her right hand and a steamy hot cup of coffee in her left. Unbeknownst to Kenji, Wanda had spotted his reflection in the robe of Lucy Nussbaum, today's Queen for a Day.

As he stealthily slipped the butcher's knife under Wanda's neck, he grabbed her head with his free hand; Wanda buried her burning Lucky Strike cigarette deep into the hand holding the knife and simultaneously threw her scalding hot cup of Joe backward into his face.

Kenji didn't know which searing pain to react to, the scorching, burning, blistering pain of his face or the white-hot, torturous agony of the burning flesh on his hand. He dropped the knife on Wanda's lap as he recoiled in pain away from the sofa. The old landlady placed the cigarette between her lips, grabbed the knife, sprung up off of the couch, and began stabbing her attacker.

"You got some nerve coming in here disrupting Queen for a Day, you cocksucker!" Wanda shouted.

The stab wounds weren't life-threatening, but since Wanda wasn't the neatest of house cleaners, he would need to be treated for tetanus. Kenji eventually regained his vision and turned around to exit the way he had entered through the kitchen. On his way out, Wanda turned the knife around to hold it by the blade and threw it as hard as she could. The blade hit its mark, sticking four inches into Kenji's back, just missing his spinal cord.

RAAAAAHHHHH!!!

Kenji reached inside his waistband, pulled out a snub-nosed pistol .38, and fired four shots, killing Wanda Wilson seconds before Bill Cullen, the host of The Price is Right, was able to introduce today's contestants.

Before leaving, Kenji gave Wanda a swift kick to her ribs, breaking three ribs. He sneered, "Bitch." He stumbled from the kitchen to the deserted parking lot where his powder blue Oldsmobile Rocket 88 Club Sedan was parked.

Because the butcher's knife was sticking out, he couldn't recline back, so he had to drive leaning forward. He kept the window rolled up, hoping that it would make it harder for anyone to see the blade protruding out his back.

Once he pulled into his garage, he sat there for several minutes until Chie came out to see what was taking him so long. Seeing him slumped over the steering wheel and the knife stuck in his back, she thought he was dead.

"Kenji," she said as she touched his shoulder.

He let out a groan and turned his scalded face to her; Chie screamed, "Kenji!"

"Help me inside."

She was thankful the garage was attached to the house so no one could see him in that condition. Chie took him into the bedroom and laid him on his stomach on the bed.

"I better call the doctor," She said.

"You can't. How can we explain the knife in my back? No, you'll have to remove it. Just grab hold and pull it out quickly. Do it!"

Chie grabbed the handle and yanked it out. The minute the knife was removed, blood began gushing out. She ran into the bathroom and grabbed a bunch of towels; then, she applied heavy pressure on the wound. The pain was so excruciating that Kenji passed out. She gently irrigated the wound and applied a clean bandage, and eventually, it stopped bleeding. She ran up to Walgreens and bought some disinfecting ointment, came back, and redressed the back wound as well as the other superficial stab slashes and the cigarette burn.

He was unconscious for eighteen hours, and when he was able to walk, she forcibly drove him to see a doctor to get a tetanus shot.

"What happened to you, Mr. Yamamoto?" Doctor Tsuri asked.

"I was attacked by some gang members last night," Yamamoto said.

"Did you call the police?"

"I did, and they filed a report. But they said I shouldn't expect them to be caught since I didn't get a good look at the punks."

"It's a shame that these thugs are roaming the streets attacking innocent people like yourself. Well, the good news is that you're going to be fine. You'll just need to take it easy for the next couple of days and keep those clean."

"Thank you, doctor."

"My nurse will be right in to give you a tetanus shot. If you have any issues, be sure to come see me."

"I will. Thanks again."

On the way home, Chie asked, "So, did you kill the old bat?"

"Yeah, after I killed the bitch, I kicked her in the ribs for good luck. I think I broke a couple because I heard them crack," He said with a chortle.

Chapter Fourteen
Waku Waku

In anticipation of further attacks, Marlboro and Wakabayashi began preparing for the storm they knew was coming.

Shortly after the debacle with the three stooges, Kobayashi made another visit to the paint store with five lackeys in tow.

"*Ohayō* (good morning), Kobayashi-san. What can we do for you today?" Marlboro asked with a slight bow.

"*Ohayō*, Baker-san," Kobayashi replied, returning the gesture.

While Marlboro engaged with Kobayashi, his goons casually walked around the store. One was even taking pictures.

Wakabayashi was standing behind the cash register, her hand resting on the Browning Automatic Rifle in case shit was getting ready to go down.

"Can I help you, gentlemen?" She asked.

"Oh, no, thank you. We are just admiring your beautiful shop," A particularly surly-looking thug replied. Even though he and the others tried to hide the fact that they were tatted from their necks down to their toes, it was obvious that they were hardcore yakuza. The one that had just spoken to her smiled, revealing his two front teeth capped in gold.

"I have found that I need five more paintbrushes, several stir sticks, and three drop cloths," Kobayashi said to Marlboro.

"Of course. Right this way, Kobayashi-san."

Marlboro gathered the materials and brought them to the register, where Wakabayashi rang up the sale.

"How's the project going," She asked.

"Very well," Kobayashi replied.

"Would you let me know how it turns out when it's all done, Kobayashi-san?" Marlboro asked.

"You will be first to know," Kobayashi said, surrounded by his five hooligans.

"Do please come again, anytime."

"Oh, rest assured, we will be back."

"I can't wait," Marlboro said brusquely.

"What do you think that was all about?" Wakabayashi asked. Marlboro once Kobayashi left.

"They were casing the joint. Looking for weak spots."

"So, Whadda think?"

"I think we better come up with some serious booby traps. Now, I got a nasty feeling that they're gearing up for an all-out assault."

"Do we need to call Detective Tanaka?"

"And tell him what? At the moment, we got nothing, just a hunch. We'll give him a call when the shit hits the fan. I'm going to give the place a once over and see that when all Hell breaks loose, there will be some surprises for our friends. You mind the store while I get things done. Holler if you need me," Marlboro said as he went downstairs into the basement.

The basement has one narrow window that a small intruder could easily access. Marlboro wielded the window shut and placed a sound alarm in case someone broke the pane of glass. He then worked on the basement staircase leading up to the main floor. Removing the original 1.5" pine tread of steps number five, seven, and ten, Marlboro replaced them with a thin 1/8" tread of plywood so that when the interloper stepped on the scraggy tread, his foot would break through, plunging his leg onto a dozen razor-sharp metal spikes. He then removed all the lightbulbs, so the basement was pitch black. On his way out of the cellar, he greased the top six treads with STP 30-weight motor oil. The metal door to the basement was bolted shut from the outside.

"Wakabayashi, whatever you do, do not go into the basement," Marlboro said.

"Why?" Wakabayashi asked.

"If you go down there, you won't be coming back up!"

As an added surprise, he filled the overhead sprinkler system with a mixture of black oil-based paint and polyacrylic adhesive.

After he accomplished that, Marlboro went upstairs to the apartment to set some traps. The first thing he did was loosen the bolts that held the fire escape to the brick façade of the building. He calculated that the structure would collapse under the weight of two adult men.

In the apartment, he painted all the windows black to block out all the light. Next, he hotwired the metal frames of the windows facing the alley and placed trays of electrified water under the windows in the living room and bedroom. If anyone stepped into the trays, they would be electrocuted. He then scattered several 'mantraps,' large mechanical steel frame traps with steel springs and sharp teeth that would crush and break the victim's leg above the ankle, throughout the living room floor.

Finally, he jimmy-rigged the landing lights from the Lockheed F-104 Starfighter to switch them on and off at irregular intervals so the intruder's eyes wouldn't be able to adjust and keep them disorientated.

The only thing he still had to do was set the boobytraps on the roof. First, he laid down several layers of fire barrier composite sheets covering the entire roof. Next, he used some Sherwin-Williams fire-resistant paint, and when that was complete, he placed several hundred spring-loaded nail and screw boards that were capable of penetrating even the thickest-soled shoes or boots.

When he was done, he went to the paint store to tell Wakabayashi of all he had accomplished.

Wakabayashi's eyes were like two large saucers. "Wow, Marlboro. It sounds like we're ready for anything."

"Yeah, I think we're good. Unless they're packing a bazooka."

"Well, why don't we lock up early, go upstairs, and show me what you're packing?" Wakabayashi said as she began to unbutton her blouse.

Marlboro smiled and said, "*Waku waku* (I'm excited)."

Detective Charlie Bell got the call that Wanda Wilson was found shot to death in her apartment. After cursing to himself, he walked down the hall to Detective Tanaka's office to let him in on the bad news.

"Hey, Sarge, got some bad news," Bell said.

"What?"

"Just got a call that Wanda Wilson was found shot to death in her apartment."

"Okay, grab your coat. Let's blow."

When they arrived at the crime scene, Officer Shackleford was joking around with Doctor Gyening, the M.E.

"What's so funny, Officer Shackleford?" Tanaka tersely asked.

"Ah, nothing, sir."

"So, why don't you go canvas the neighborhood and see what you can find out."

"Yes, sir."

"Whatta we got, Doc?"

"Well, as you can see, the old gal looks like she gave as good as she got. From what I can glean is that she must have been sitting on the couch watching TV when the assailant snuck up on her with a knife that he had taken from the butcher's block. I think she probably burned him with a cigarette."

"How can you tell that?" Bell asked.

"See the cigarette butt there on the floor; it looks like it's been snubbed out, and it has a faint odor of burnt flesh. Also, see the spilled coffee behind the couch; it's like she was seated and threw the cup of coffee up and behind her, possibly hitting him in the face. And finally, since we didn't find the missing knife, she might have stabbed the intruder with it. See, the blood splatter over by the door; the pattern doesn't suggest it came from her gunshot wounds, so I'm assuming that it might have come from the killer," Gyening explained.

"Charlie, call around to all the ERs and doctor's offices and see if anybody's been treated for burns, scalding, or stabbings," Tanaka said.

"Right, Sarge."

"Doctor Tsuri's office."

"Hello, this is Detective Bell of the LAPD. I was hoping that you might be able to help me. Had you recently treated a patient for either a minor burn, possible scalding of the facial area, or a knife wound?"

"One moment, I'll let you speak with Doctor Tsuri's nurse."

Minutes passed before he heard, "Detective Bell, this is Doctor Tsuri's nurse, Miss Kurusu; how may I help you?"

"I am calling to see if you had recently treated a patient for either a minor burn, possible scalding of the facial area, or a knife wound?"

"As a matter of fact, we did. Yesterday, a Mister Kenji Yamamoto came in with a stab wound of the upper back. He said that he received it when some members of a street gang attacked him."

"Why, might I ask, you didn't report it to the police?"

"He told us that he had already reported it to the police," The nurse said.

"Oh, I see. Well, I think it best that you don't rely on the patient's word and report such wounds yourself from now on."

"I'm so sorry, Detective. I will be sure to do that from now on. I hope I didn't mess anything up for you."

"No, it's fine. I appreciate your help, Nurse Kurusu. Goodbye."

"Goodbye, Detective Bell.

CLICK.

Detective Sergeant Tanaka, Detective Juneau, and Detective Bell arrived at Kenji Yamamoto's home. They had requested three uniformed officers and were surprised to find Officer Rusty Shackleford waiting for them.

"Shackleford, what are you doing here? I didn't request you." Tanaka asked.

"I heard the call. I was in the neighborhood, so I thought I might be able to assist." He said.

"Okay, you wait out here as backup."

"Are you sure, sir?"

"I'm sure."

Tanaka had a nailing feeling, an uneasy intuition about Officer Shackleford, but he had nothing to base it on- just a gut feeling. But sometimes, you have to go with your gut.

Once the house was surrounded, Tanaka rang the doorbell. An attractive Japanese woman answered the door. Tanaka held his badge and announced, "I'm Detective Sergeant Tanaka. I have a warrant to search your house. Is your husband home?"

"Yes, but he's not feeling well," She said.

"Where would I find him?"

"In the bedroom. But he's not feeling well."

"That's all right; we have brought a doctor to ensure he is being looked after. I must insist you stay in the living room with Officer Pam Ellis."

Tanaka said to the police photographer, Be sure you document everything. Got that?"

"Got it!"

The three detectives and a police doctor entered the master bedroom, where they found Kenji Yamamoto lying on his side, fast asleep.

"Kenji Yamamoto, you're under arrest for the murder of Wanda Wilson," Tanaka said.

Yamamoto was disorientated as he sat up; Detective Juneau put handcuffs on the suspect; after he was in custody, the doctor examined the wound on his back.

"That's a nasty stab wound you have there, Mister Yamamoto. How did you get that?" Tanaka asked.

"I was attacked by a bunch of gang members the day before yesterday."

"Yeah, that's what Doctor Tsuri's nurse told us. But as hard as I tried, I couldn't find any police report you told her you had made." Detective Bell said.

"It must have fallen between the cracks," Yamamoto explained.

Say, how did you come by that cigarette burn on the top of your hand?" Tanaka asked.

"I fell asleep while smoking."

"And did you fall asleep at the dining room table and plopped your face into a boiling bowl of miso soup, too?"

"Yeah, I've been working very hard at the office."

"And what do you do?"

"I'm in finance."

"What's the name of the company?" Tanaka asked.

"Kobayashi Financial Group."

"Would that be the same Kobayashi that heads up the Black Rain?"

"Black Rain? I don't know any Black Rain."

"Yeah, sure. Come on. We're going down to the station."

As they were escorting the prisoner to a squad car, one of the police officers came up to them, holding a butcher's knife. "Detective, look what we found."

"Where did you find it?" Tanaka asked.

"It was in the garbage can outside." He said.

"Tag it and bag it. And don't let anyone but you handle it," Bell ordered.

"Yes, sir."

Once Yamamoto was placed in the detective's car, another officer announced that they had discovered a .38 snub-nosed pistol.

"That's not mine! You planted that gun. Chie, call Kobayashi-san and tell him that I've been arrested!" Yamamoto shouted.

Chapter Fifteen
Kenji Yamamoto

"When am I going to get the rest of the men you promised, Hanzō?" Kobayashi demanded.

Hanzō Doumekii, the *oyabun* of the San Francisco chapter of Black Rain, had decided it was easier to send Kobayashi some more men rather than having this continuous bickering and whining.

"Kio, do not worry. I am sending down five of my very best men. They should arrive this afternoon."

"I hope they aren't planning on getting into a gun battle on the way down," Kobayashi said sarcastically.

CLICK.

"Kobayashi-san, that Police Officer Shackleford is outside. He said that you wanted to see him," said Arata, Kobayashi's lackey.

"Send him in."

Kobayashi sat at the *chabudai,* reviewing some financial documents without giving any notice when Officer Shackleford entered the room.

Shackleford gave a slight bow out of respect, then stood silently, hat in hand, waiting.

Without looking up, Kobayashi gruffly asked, "What is it you want?"

"You wanted to see me."

Kobayashi said nothing; he continued studying his financial documents for another ten minutes, leaving Shackleford standing before him.

Finally, Kobayashi looked up, "I hear that Kenji Yamamoto has been arrested for murder."

"That's right; he was arrested for the killing of that old woman who was the eyewitness that was going to testify against him."

"I want him released."

"Release him?"

"That wasn't a question. That was an order."

"How can I do that?"

"That's your problem."

"You must be joking!" Shackleford said.

"Officer Shackleford, do you know who these gentlemen are?" Kobayashi said, referring to Chiharu Toyoda, Kazz Daguchi, and Yuuma Hagihara, who entered the room.

"Yeah, I know them. Those are your henchmen."

"That is correct. They will come to visit you if you fail to free Kenji Yamamoto from his incarceration within the next three days. Just remember, Officer Shackleford, you sought me out. I have paid you a substantial advance, have I not?"

"Yes, but..."

"Three days, *sayōnara*, Officer Shackleford," Kobayashi said, returning to his paperwork. The three henchmen walked him out.

Arata entered Kobayashi's office, bowed, and announced that the new men from San Francisco had arrived.

"Do you want to meet them, Kobayashi-san?"

"I do not. Have them report to Chiharu Toyoda."

"*Hai.*"

Chiharu Toyoda was sitting in the lobby of Kobayashi Financial Group when Arata brought the five new men down to him.

"I was told that these men were to report to you."

"Yeah, who told you that?"

"Kobayashi."

"Ah, great. Okay, listen up, you *panko* (punks), follow me; we're going for a little ride," Toyoda said as he led them out into the parking garage, where they all piled into a black Lincoln Continental Mark III.

Toyoda got behind the wheel and drove to the *Natsukashī Kokoro* paint store. He parked the black behemoth directly across the street so they could observe their target.

"Don't let the name fool you; five good men died in that paint store trying to kill the owners. An ex-GI and his whore of a wife. That will be our target when the time comes. See that guy putting up the display sign? That's Butch Baker and the Japanese bitch next to him; that's his whore, Aiko," Toyoda said.

"Why don't we just go in there right now and blast the shit out of them both?" Atsuki Ryujin, one of the newbies, asked.

"The place is like Fort Knox. The front door is electronically locked, the window glass is bulletproof, and don't you think we haven't already tried that, *kuso yarō* (asshole)?"

"So, why are we here if not to attack this *gaijin* and his whore?" Ryujin asked.

"Man, you're dumber than you look. We're here to case the joint and find any weak points. Now, let's go around back to the alley and see if there's anything there," Toyoda said.

When they parked directly behind the paint store, Toyoda told Ryujin, who weighed all of one hundred pounds, to see if he thought he could squeeze in through the basement window. Ryujin got down on his hands and knees and peered into the casement. He turned to the Lincoln and gave a thumbs up as he ran back.

"No sweat, man," Ryujin said.

"Could you see anything?" Toyoda asked.

"Nah, It was pitch black."

"Okay. When the time comes, while we send some of our guys up the fire escape, you'll be sneaking in through the basement."

"How about attacking from the roof?" Isao Kombu, another of the new men, suggested.

Toyoda got out of the car and saw that some men could repel down from the hotel next door to the paint store and conceivably enter from above.

"Good thinking, kid. Let's head back to HQ," Toyoda said as he got back into the car.

"Officer Shackleford to see prisoner Kenji Yamamoto."

The duty officer shoved the sign-in log toward Shackleford and said, "Sign here. Lock your weapon in the locker and wait to be buzzed in."

Shackleford did as he was told; as he waited for Yamamoto to be brought into the visitor's area, he was aware that surveillance cameras were recording him. But he had no choice but to take the risk.

BUZZZZZ

"Shackleford. Have you come to get me out?" Yamamoto asked, speaking into the telephone receiver.

"I'm working on it, Kenji. Jesus, what the fuck happened to you?"

His face was bloody and swollen, having been beaten by his cellmate, Jimmy "the Shiv" Nussbaum, who wanted him to perform oral sex. When he refused, his 'cellie' slammed his face into the concrete wall, knocking him unconscious, turning him on his stomach, and 'boofing' him in the ass.

"My cellmate beat me up for not blowing him."

He opened his mouth to show Shackleford that three teeth had been knocked out.

"Fuck me. Try and stay away from him the best you can. And if you can't, maybe next time you should go ahead and blow the guy," Shackleford chuckled.

"Very funny, asshole. I'd like to see how you handle yourself when you land your ass in prison!" Yamamoto barked.

"Yeah, that ain't going to happen. You need to just hang in there for a couple of days. I'm working on a plan."

"Hurry up, I don't know how much longer I can survive," Yamamoto pleaded.

"Okay, I got to scoot. Remember, don't say nothing to nobody. Just keep your mouth shut. Especially with your 'cellie,'" Shackleford smirked as he hung up the phone and left.

CLICK.

"Did you get all of that?" Detective Sergeant Tanaka asked prison guard Wally Hampton when he turned off the recording device.

"Yes, sir. I'll play it back for you," Hampton said.

"Shackleford. Have you come to get me out?"

"I'm working on it, Kenji. Jesus, what the fuck happened to you?"

"My cellmate beat me up for not blowing him."

"Fuck me. Try and stay away from him the best you can. And if you can't, maybe next time you should go ahead and blow the guy."

"Very funny, asshole. I'd like to see how you handle yourself when you land your ass in prison!"

"Yeah, that ain't going to happen. You need to just hang in there for a couple of days. I'm working on a plan."
"Hurry up; I don't know how much longer I can survive."

"Okay, I got to scoot. Remember, don't say nothing to nobody. Just keep your mouth shut. Especially with your 'cellie.'"

"Great. Make me two copies and send them to my office," Tanaka said.

Shackleford didn't notice the two plainclothes police officers following him as he left Rikers Island prison.

Officer Shackleford hadn't lied to Kenji Yamamoto when he told him he had a plan to get him out of prison. He had a plan; he had arranged for Jimmy "the Shiv" Nussbaum to be Yamamoto's cellmate. Nussbaum was convicted of murdering his wife with a meat cleaver. He chopped her up into bite-size chunks and fed her to his two Rottweilers, Fritz and Snooky.

He received his nickname, "the Shiv," for stabbing to death five fellow prisoners with homemade shivs. When asked why he did it, he said, "I like to watch them die."

The Shiv is currently serving six life sentences with no chance of parole, so Shackleford secretly arranged with a pal, Rob Ackley, who's a Riker's prison guard, to have Nussbaum transferred into Yamamoto's cell; it cost him five hundred dollars still leaving him a cool forty-five hundred bucks profit from the 5Gs that Yamamoto had given him.

Nussbaum had all of his victims' names tattooed on his right arm, like the notches on the Old West's gunfighter pistols. Shackleford figured it was just a matter of time before Yamamoto would be tattoo number seven, and he was right.

Shortly after Shackleford's visit, Yamamoto returned to his cell; his cellmate wasn't there, much to the relief of Yamamoto. Nussbaum was watching Yamamoto, waiting for the perfect opportunity to strike. It came when Yamamoto was sitting on the toilet. Nussbaum calmly walked into the cell, Shiv in hand, and began stabbing Yamamoto with his pants down around his ankles. The prison doctor counted over forty stab wounds, and Yamamoto's throat had been cut, his eyes gouged out, and his testicles were removed and stuffed in Yamamoto's mouth.

When asked why he did it. Nussbaum answered, "Fucking Japs. Remember Pearl Harbor."

"Were you in the war?"

"Naw. They rejected me and classified me as "4Γ." They thought I was mentally and morally unfit to go and kill people. Pretty funny, huh? When can I go? I got to see about getting a tattoo," Nussbaum chortled.

Chapter Sixteen
Night Visitors

Marlboro and Wakabayashi had both fallen asleep naked after having sex on the sofa. They probably would have continued sleeping there if it hadn't been for the basement alarm, followed by the frightful muffled screams emanating from below.

Marlboro bolted off from the sofa, jumped into his chinos lying on the floor, put on a pair of steel-toed boots, grabbed his Ithaca Model 1911 A1 .45 pistol and an Eveready 9100 Lantern Battery Flashlight, and ran downstairs to the basement.

Since he had taken all the lightbulbs out of the basement several days before, he was aware that whoever was screaming in agony must have stepped on the boobytrap and plunged their foot onto the sharp barbed metal spikes. As Marlboro got closer to the basement door, the screams grew louder.

EEEYAAAAA!!!

Marlboro kept the lights off in the hallway so that when he did open the door, he wouldn't be a backlit silhouette target standing in the doorway. He stood to one side of the door, turned on the flashlight, placed it on the ground, aimed the beam so it would shine down onto the basement stairs, and then slowly opened the door. Just as he suspected, the intruder instinctively popped off two rounds.

KA-POW! POW!

"Drop the gun!" Marlboro shouted.

"*Fakkuyū (fuck you)!*"

"Okay," Marlboro said as he closed the door.

"Come back!"

Once again, Marlboro slowly opened the door, standing off to one side.

"Throw your weapon up here and put your hands up!" Marlboro ordered.

Seconds later, a Nambu Type 14 .8mm pistol was tossed up onto the landing.

"Help me. I am unarmed," The voice said.

Marlboro, not taking any chances, held a small mirror angled down to see if the culprit, with his hands above his head, was indeed unarmed. The would-be assassin was holding a Type 2 Hamada Semi-Automatic Pistol.

Marlboro slammed the door shut, "*Sayōnara*, baby!"

The hitman fired six shots at the metal door, none of them penetrating it. Marlboro could hear the screams continue, as well as a few Japanese curse words that he wasn't familiar with. One in particular, *hahaoya baka*.

He trotted back upstairs, where Wakabayashi was hanging up the phone.

"Who did you call?" Her asked.

"Detective Tanaka. He's on his way."

"Ambulance?"

"Yeah, I told him to be sure to have one."

"He's going to need one, for sure," Marlboro said.

"How's our guest?" Wakabayashi asked.

"Not at all thrilled. He actually tried to trick me with the old 'I'm unarmed, come save me' routine."

"Well, that was unthoughtful."

"By the way, what does *hahaoya baka* mean?"

"Mother fucker."

"Well, that wasn't a very nice thing to say," Marlboro grinned.

A few minutes later, they heard the sound of police and ambulance sirens downstairs, followed by banging on the shop's front door. Wakabayashi opened the door and let Detective Tanaka, three uniformed police officers, and two EMT medics enter.

"Where is he, Marlboro?" Detective Tanaka asked.

"He's stuck in the basement."

"Stuck?" What do you mean stuck?"

"You'll see. We'll need the medic, too," Marlboro said.

They followed Marlboro to the basement landing, where he slightly cracked the metal door, just enough so the intruder could hear him.

"Hello. The police and a couple of medics are here," Marlboro hollered.

The trapped killer fired our shots, ricocheting off the metal door.

PWIING! PWIING! PWIING! PWIING!

Tanaka shouted, "If you don't surrender, I'm going to lob some tear gas in there."

"*Fakkuyū (fuck you)!*"

"That's what he said to me," Marlboro said.

"Fire one down there," Tanaka ordered Officer Jackson, holding the tear gas rife.

Marlboro opened the metal door just enough for the tear gas muzzle to fit. Jackson squeezed the trigger and fired.

BLAM! HISSS-SSS-SSSSS

It didn't take long before they heard the sound of gagging and coughing.

AAAGGGHHH! KOFF. KOFF.

"I give up! Open the door. I surrender!"

Marlboro gestured for everyone to stand clear of the door. He opened the door and shouted, "Throw up your weapon. Now!"

A Type 2 Hamada Semi-Automatic Pistol was thrown onto the landing. When Marlboro peered in, he saw a young Japanese man who looked to be in his twenties holding his hands above his head, tears streaming down his face.

"I better lead the way; there are a couple of booby traps you'll want to avoid," Marlboro said.

The medics weren't able to extricate the would-be assassin's foot from the barbed metal spikes at the scene, so they brought the whole board that the mini harpoons were attached to out with him. They would have to be removed at the hospital.

"How is he, Doc?" Tanaka asked the chief medic.

"He's fine. However, he might lose the foot. We'll know when we get him to the hospital."

Tanaka stepped into the ambulance with the intruder while one of the medics was about to administer some pain medication.

Tanaka asked, "What's your name?"

The man snapped, "*Fakkuyū.*"

"Hold off on that painkiller," Tanaka said, squeezing the man's foot hard.

"*YEAAAAARGH!*

"I said, what's your name?"

"Atsuki Ryujin," He said, whimpering.

"Now, that wasn't so hard, was it? Okay, Doc, go ahead.

Moments later, Ryujin conked out from the painkiller. An officer handcuffed him to the gurney and escorted him to the prison hospital,

Up in Marlboro and Wakabayashi's apartment above the paint store, Tanaka asked, "Okay, what happened?"

"We were snoozing here on the sofa when we heard the alarm Marlboro had installed in the basement; then there was this awful screaming. So, that's when we knew we had an intruder," Wakabayashi explained.

Marlboro continued, "Yeah, so I ran downstairs and found that kid screaming. I offered to get him out, but he began shooting at me. I told him he could rot down there if he didn't toss up his weapon, which he did, but I figured he had another piece. I asked him to give that one up, too, and that's when he began to shoot at me again. So, I said, fuck it, came upstairs, and had Wakabayashi call you. By the way, here's his pistols," Marlboro said as he handed the gats over to Tanaka.

"Hmm, a Type 2 Hamada Semi-Automatic Pistol and a Nambu Type 14 .8mm pistol. Both Imperial Japanese Army issued. Thanks," Tanaka said.

"Well, I better go downstairs, repair that window, hook up the alarm, and re-booby trap those stairs," Marlboro said.

On his way out, Tanaka took the roscoes with him. He spied a pair of lace panties, turned, and said, smirking, "Snoozing. Right!"

Chapter Seventeen
Fireball

"You wanted to see me?" Officer Shackleford asked.

"I just received word that Kenji Yamamoto was been murdered in prison," Kobayashi said.

Shackleford feigned surprise, "No shit! What happened?"

"Apparently, a guard placed Kenji in with a cellmate who has a record of torturing and killing fellow inmates."

"That's terrible."

"Yes, it is. I believe I had asked you to obtain a release for Kenji, did I not?"

"Yes, you did, and I was working on a plan to get him out."

"I would like you to come with me," Kobayashi said as he stood from his *chabudai* and gestured for Shackleford to follow. Chiharu Toyoda and Kazz Daguchi escorted their *oyabun* and the *gaijin* to the basement, where a hooded man sat tied to a wooden chair. His head leaned forward, suggesting that he was either sleeping or unconscious.

Police Officer Rusty Shackleford had a bad feeling in the pit of his stomach. As he was about to ease his hand onto his Colt – Police .38 Special, Kazz Daguchi slapped his hand away and removed the gat from its holster.

Kobayashi gave Toyoda a nod, and he snatched the covering off of the hooded man's head, revealing it to be Correctional Officer Rob Ackley, who, by the looks of him, had been severely beaten. His eyes were swollen shut; blood streamed from his mouth, and he had been garroted to death.

"Officer Shackleford, this was Correctional Officer Ackley. He admitted before he died that you had paid him five hundred dollars to have Kenji placed in the same cell as Jimmy "the Shiv" Nussbaum. Is that true?" Kobayashi asked.

"No! That's crazy. Why would I do that? I was about to get him out," Shackleford said.

"Ah, yes. So you said but never explained how you would achieve his release. So, please be so kind as to tell me now how you would get him out."

"Well. I ah. You see. I was going to…" Shackleford stammered. Then everything went black as Chiharu Toyoda sapped Shackleford on the back of his head, rendering him unconscious. When he awoke, he found himself tied to a wooden chair next to the body of Correctional Officer Ackley. Sitting across from him was Chiharu, "the *Gorira* (gorilla)" Toyoda. He smiled when he saw Shackleford was awake; Toyoda stood up, slipped on a pair of brass knuckles, and before Shackleford could utter a word, smashed his fist into the police officer's mouth, knocking out all of his front teeth with a single blow.

AAARRRRGGGGHHHHH!

Next came a series of body blows that broke eight ribs, the sternum, both clavicles, and his right humerus.

YEEEEAAAHHHH! EEEYYARRGGGGHH!

"That's enough," Kobayashi said, sitting off to one side and watching the beating joyfully.

Shackleford sat writhing in pain, breathing heavily, trying to gather his thoughts. He looked over to Kobayashi, spit out a mouthful of blood, and mumbled, "You'll never get away with killing a cop!"

Kobayashi smiled, "Oh, I'm not going to kill a cop. No, you're going to die in a fiery crash as a result of drunk driving along with your friend."

Toyoda held his head back while Daguchi poured two bottles of vodka down Shackleford's throat. They then dragged him upstairs and drove him out to Laurel Canyon, rigged the car to burst into flames, and rolled Shackleford's 1950 Dodge Coronet Club Coupe down the hillside with Officer Shackleford conked out behind the wheel next to Officer Ackley.

When the Dodge finally stopped striking a tree, it sat for several minutes, then detonated into a giant fireball. Black smoke could be seen for miles around. The police and the fire department were there in less than ten minutes. To their surprise, one of the occupants was still alive, although badly burnt and in severe trauma, and the passenger was dead, burnt beyond recognition.

"I don't see why I have to go to the prison hospital," Marlboro said.

"I need you to ID the suspect," Tanaka explained.

"You were there. As well as the medics and a bunch of uniforms."

"Yes, but he was in your basement."

"Fine. When do you want to go?"

"Now is as good of a time as any."

"I don't like the idea of Hana being here all alone."

"I'll have Detective Juneau stay with her until you return."

"Thanks. Let's roll," Marlboro said.

On the way to the hospital, Tanaka asked, "That was a pretty nasty booby trap you set up in the basement. Are there other surprises that you set up?"

"Oh, yeah. Be sure to tell your men not to go wandering around unescorted. It could prove lethal."

"You're not serious."

"Deadly," Marlboro said.

At the hospital, they found Atsuki Ryujin sleeping, handcuffed to the bed. There was a small tent over his right leg covering his foot. Doctor Webb was standing at the bedside reviewing the case notes.

"Hey, Doc, how's he doing?" Tanaka whispered, not wanting to wake Ryujin.

"Let's go out into the hall," Doc Webb said.

Once outside the room, Webb said, "We couldn't save the foot. We had to take it off above the ankle."

"Does Ryujin know?" Marlboro asked.

"Not yet. I decided to wait until he was stronger. He's lost a lot of blood."

"Won't he know when he wakes up?" Tanaka asked.

"No. The mind plays tricks, and he will actually feel as if his foot itches; even when he sees that it's gone, he won't believe it."

"Thanks, Doc," Tanaka said.

When Marlboro and Tanaka returned to Ryujin's room, he was awake.

"How are you feeling?" Marlboro asked.

"I should have killed you when I had the chance!"

"You never had the chance, dipshit."

"You better watch your back because when I get out, I'll get you."

"I doubt it," Marlboro said.

"Who are you working for, Ryujin? Kobayashi?" Tanaka asked.

"Never heard of him, ya dirty screw," Ryujin snarled.

"Ah, a tough guy. Listen, Ryujin, I fear your crime spree is over," Tanaka said.

"I'll be out of the joint before you know it."

"You don't understand, kid. You lost your foot. The Doc couldn't save it. It was too messed up, and you had lost a lot of blood," Tanaka explained.

"You're lying; I can feel it; it itches bad. Look, I'm wriggling my toes. Go ahead and take a look!"

Tanaka pulled back the tent covering his leg and revealed that his foot was indeed gone.

Noooooooooooooo!

"Sorry, kid. Tough break," Tanaka said as he covered the leg up; Ryujin began to weep.

"What am I going to do?"

"There's plenty of things you can do, kid," Marlboro said.

"Oh, sure, I can be a cripple newsie or a beggar on street corners."

"There are plenty of trades you can learn in prison," Tanaka said.

"Yeah, like what?"

"You can learn sewing, woodworking, electronics, or auto mechanics," Tanaka said.

"So, how many years am I looking at?"

"Well, you got your breaking and entering, attempted murders of a civilian and police officers, as well as your parole violation. So, I'm guessing a minimum of fifteen, maybe twenty. But with good behavior, you could be out in less than ten," Tanaka said.

"*Fakkumī* (fuck me)."

"Take it easy, kid. At least you won't end up dead like the rest of Kobayashi's goons," Marlboro said.

"You don't know what Kobayashi has in store for you, *gaijin*!"

"As a matter of fact, I do. It's Kobayashi and his thugs, who are in store for a surprise, as were you, kid," Marlboro said with a wolfish grin.

As Tanaka and Marlboro were leaving the prison hospital, Detective Tanaka received a message that Officer Shackleford had been in an accident and was currently in the Los Angeles County Hospital burn unit.

"Shackleford has been in an accident. He's in a bad way. I have to head over to the County Hospital burn unit."

"I'll go with you," Marlboro said.

When they arrived, they were met by Officer Roger Everhart, a motorcycle cop who was one of the first on the scene.

"Hey, Roger," Tanaka said.

"Hey, Detective, Marlboro."

"Hey, Roger," Marlboro said.

"What do you know?" Tanaka asked.

"Got a call about an explosion down in Laurel Canyon. When I arrived, I saw a Dodge Coronet Club Coupe engulfed in flames. I could see two bodies trapped in the car; shortly after I got there, the fire department quickly put out the fire and pulled out two bodies; both were burnt to a crisp. Amazingly, Shackleford was somehow still alive, and the other was Correctional Officer Rob Ackley, who was pronounced dead at the scene."

"Do they know if Shackleford is going to make it?"

"They say he has a better chance of dying than he does of living. They say he's got third-degree burns over 90% of his body. I can't imagine what kind of life he will have if he does live," Everhart said.

"Do we know what caused the accident?"

"It looks like he was drunk as a skunk. His blood alcohol level was .30."

"Jeez! What does the fire department think was the cause of the explosion?"

"The 'Red Hats' are still looking into it."

"Okay, what room is he in?"

"409."

"Thanks."

When they walked into room 409, it looked like something from one of those Mummy movies. Shackleford was wrapped from head to toe in white gauze bandages. He had tubes emanating from his nose and mouth and three IVs into his arm. He was hooked up to several machines that emitted all kinds of beeps, boops, bings, bonks, and balops. A large plastic sheet separated the room so germs wouldn't be transferred to the patient.

A nurse dressed in what looked to be a hazmat suit came into the room to administer an injection through one of his IVs.

"How's he doing?" Tanaka asked.

"It's a miracle that he's still alive," She said.

"Will he live?"

"Honestly, I doubt it. But stranger things have happened. Now, I must ask you to leave."

"If there's any change at all, please have someone contact me. I'm Detective Sergeant Tanaka."

"I will."

When Kobayashi got word that the Shackleford hit was botched, he freaked out.

"What was he thinking?" Kobayashi shrieked.

"I don't know. I told him not to go off halfcocked," Toyoda said.

"From what I gathered, he's in the prison hospital, having lost his foot. The fool! And to make matters worse. I hear that Shackleford is still alive. How could you have fucked up this up?"

"There's no way he's going to survive. It's just a matter of time, *oyabun*."

"Time! He could live long enough to put us all in the electric chair, you *baka* (idiot)! I want him dead. Do you understand?"

"*Hai*."

"You fuck this up! You don't come back!"

Chapter Eighteen
Clean Up on Aisle 4

"Hey, boss, Doctor Gyening is on line one," Detective Bell shouted from the squad room.

"The M.E.? What does he want?" Tanaka asked.

"He didn't say."

Tanaka picked up the receiver and punched the blinking light.

"Tanaka."

"Detective, I think you should come down to the morgue. There's something you need to see. It's about Shackleford's crash," Doctor Gyening said.

"I'll be there as soon as I can."

CLICK

When Tanaka arrived, Doctor Gyening was waiting in the lobby, having a cigarette and joking with a couple of the lab rats. Doctor Gyening refers to his assistants as lab rats.

"Ah, Detective Sergeant Tanaka, thanks for coming," Gyening said.

"Whatta got, Doc."

"It's Correctional Officer Rob Ackley."

"What about him?" Tanaka asked.

"He didn't die in the car crash; he was murdered."

"What? How?"

"He was garroted."

"Are you sure? But I thought he was burned beyond recognition."

"You want to come see for yourself?"

"Ah, no thanks. I'll take your word for it. Burnt bodies freak me out ever since I liberated Auschwitz," Tanaka said.

"Quite understandable."

"So, there's a good chance Shackleford's crash was staged to look like a drunk driving accident in hopes that he would be killed. If that's the case, I better get an officer at the hospital. Conceivably, someone might want to finish the job. I need to use your phone, Doc," Tanaka said.

"It's over on my desk."

"Hello, Charlie. It's me. Get a uniform over to the hospital right away and have them babysit Shackleford. Nobody goes in except the nurses and the doctors. It turns out Ackley was murdered, and there may be an attempt on Shackleford's life. Meet me at the hospital."

"Right, boss."

CLICK

Detective Juneau went to the prison hospital to interview Atsuki Ryujin. He found him staring off into space, a product of having been heavily dosed with large quantities of morphine.

"Atsuki, I'm Detective Juneau. Feel like talking?" Juneau asked.

"Sure, man. Why not."

"Great. I just need some information. What's your full name?"

"Atsuki Ryujin."

"How old are you?"

"Twenty-two"

"Where were you born?"

"San Francisco."

"What's your current address?"

"The Taiheiyo Hotel. On the corner of Weller and South San Pedro."

"How long have you lived there?"

"Six weeks."

"Before that? Where did you live?"

"San Francisco."

"Why did you move here?"

"A job."

"What do you do for a living?"

"I'm a yakuza."

"What were you doing in the basement of the paint store?"

"I went there to kill the *gaijin* and the whore. I would have to if I hadn't stepped on the boob trap!"

"Why did you want to kill Butch Baker and his wife?"

"For my *oyabun*."

"And who's your *oyabun*?"

"Kio Kobayashi."

"Did Kio Kobayashi send you to kill the Bakers?"

"No. I wanted to impress my *oyabun*. But I failed. I must now make amends to him."

"How will you do that?"

"*Yubitsume*."

"*Yubitsume*? What is *yubitsume*?"

Ryujin did not answer; he just stared off into nothingness. Finally, he uttered, "Go."

Tanaka rushed over to the Los Angeles County Hospital burn unit, where Officer Pete Bisbee sat outside Shackleford's room.

"Anything to report?" Tanaka asked.

"No, sir. Since I've been here, no one has entered the room."

Down in the hospital lobby, Chiharu Toyoda, dressed in a lightweight London Fog jacket, stood looking at the direction board when a doctor dressed in blue scrubs passed by.

"Excuse me, doctor, a relative of mine was in an auto accident. He's badly burned. Could you please tell me where I can find him?" Toyoda asked.

The doctor replied, "You should ask at the Reception Desk."

"There's no one there, Doctor."

"Well, he would probably be in the burn unit on the fourth floor."

"Thank you, doctor," Toyoda said as he made his way to the stairs.

The doctor wouldn't have given it another thought, except the hospital was abuzz with a policeman sitting outside a burn victim who was involved in an auto accident. He walks to the reception desk, picks up the phone, and dials the number to the burn unit.

The nurse at the desk answered, "Hello, burn unit." She listens, then leans over the desk. She sees Tanaka talking to the officer and says, holding the phone up, "For you, Detective Tanaka."

"Hello, Detective Tanaka."

"This is Doctor Kenny. It may be nothing, but a man just asked me where he could find a relative who was in a fiery car crash. I thought you might want to know."

"Was he Japanese?"

"Uh-huh. I'm afraid I told him he'd be on the fourth floor. I didn't think."

"Thanks, Doctor," Tanaka said as he returned the phone to the nurse.

"What's up, sir?" Officer Bisbee asked.

"I think there's a hatchet man here to knock off, Shackleford. He was tipped where to find him."

"Radio in and get some uniforms down here ASAP. Get in the room with Shackleford, and don't let anybody in except the Doctor and the nurses. Nobody!"

"Yes, sir."

Chiharu Toyoda climbed the sixty stairs to the fourth floor without being seen. He stopped to catch his breath and removed a nine-inch wooden handled *aisupikku* (ice pick) he had tapped around his ankle. He then eases the fireproof door open to see if the coast is clear. He sees the nurse's station is busy with nurses giving out medication and food services handing out food trays. As luck would have it, the nurse's lounge is directly across from the stairwell. When he thinks it's safe, he darts across the hall and into the lounge, where he changes into a pair of ill-fitting scrubs.

When he came out of the lounge, Tanaka immediately spotted him, who pulled out his revolver, aimed, and shouted, "Drop your weapon!"

Toyoda was fortunate that Nurse Sarah Tyne happened to be walking by. He grabbed her and placed the icepick to her neck, and answered, "Put the gun down, copper, or the bitch dies!"

"Ain't going to happen. Just let the nice nurse go."

Tanaka held the gun up to take a shot when a doctor shouted, "You can't fire a gun in here; the whole floor is filled with pure oxygen. The whole place will go up in flames."

"Hear that copper! Now, me and the nice nursey here are going to waltz out of here. Once I'm outside, I'll let her go. Got it? If you try anything funny, she dies."

Meantime, Marlboro was in the paint store dealing with the owner of the Mikado Hotel, who was renovating and refreshing the place by bringing in new furniture and carpets and painting all of the rooms. Little did Marlboro know that the Black Rain was funding the project to gain access to the rooms overlooking the *Natsukashī Kokoro's* roof.

Watanabe had just gotten out of the shower upstairs when she accidentally slipped and started to fall. Instinctively, she grabbed the shower curtain, which helped break her fall, but in doing so, she twisted her left ankle. She lay there naked, soaking wet, and embarrassed.

Downstairs, Marlboro heard the thump from above when she hit the floor. Since he didn't hear her call out, he continued with the sale. Once the business was concluded, he put the "will return in fifteen minutes" sign in the window and went upstairs to see what had happened.

"Watanabe, is everything all right?" He called out.

"Marlboro, I could use some help."

He entered the bathroom and found her lying on the floor, all wet and naked.

"Mmm, kinky," He said, smiling.

"I twisted my ankle."

He could see the ankle had begun to swell up; it was the size of a softball.

"I see. Wanna fool around?" He said with a devilish grin.

"No! You're such a jerk."

"Okay, bye." He said as he began to turn to leave.

"Marlboro, get your ass in here. I need to get to the ER. Help me get dressed."

"Actually, I'm better at helping you get undressed."

Watanabe shot him such a dirty look that he knew if he ever wanted to see her naked again, he better do what she wanted, and quickly.

After she was dressed, he carried her downstairs, out the front door, and into the car. Then, off they went to L.A. County Hospital.

"See, that's why we should always shower together," Marlboro said seriously.

With her hair still wet, she smiled and said, "Oh, you'd like that."

"Well, I'm only thinking of your safety."

"Uh, huh. I bet that's what you were thinking of."

"If I'm in there with you. You can have something to grab on."

She gave a glance at his crotch and said, "Yeah, I know exactly what you'd want me to grab on. You perv."

"Watanabe! Get your mind out of the gutter."

When they reached the hospital, Marlboro pulled up to the ER and ran in to get a wheelchair. He helped his partner into the chair and wheeled her into the lobby.

"Sit tight; I'll be right back. Just have to park the car."

"Okay."

When he returned, she was already filling out the paperwork to get the long, arduous process started of waiting hours to be attended to.

As they were waiting, Marlboro noticed a swarm of uniforms rushing into the hospital. He flagged down someone he knew of the force.

"Charlie! What's going on?"

"Tanaka called in that there was a possible 133 up in the burn unit."

Not having brought his gun, Marlboro looked around for something to use as a weapon. He spotted and grabbed a mop and pail sitting in a corner and headed to the stairwell.

Watanabe snickered, "What are you planning to do with that? Clean up the mess on aisle four?"

"Exactly!"

When Marlboro reached the fourth floor, he cracked open the stairwell door to find some guy in scrubs holding something up to a nurse's throat. Down the hall, he saw Tanaka aiming his pistol at the suspect. More and more officers were arriving at the scene every minute.

Marlboro opened the door, placed the pail on the ground, and began to mop the floor. Toyoda spun around and shouted, "What the fuck do you think you're doing!"

"I'm just doing my job, man," Marlboro said innocently.

"Step away from the door, asshole!"

"Yes, sir," Marlboro said as he eased away from the stairwell.

As Toyoda and his hostage slowly sidestepped toward the exit, Marlboro got into position.

"Don't try anything cute, or she gets this icepick in her gullet. Got it?"

"Gullet. Got it." Marlboro nodded.

"Oh, a wise guy, huh? Say you look familiar. Do I know you?"

"Ah, I don't think so," Marlboro replied.

"Step back!"

When Toyoda was preoccupied reaching behind him to open the door, Marlboro knocked over the pail full of soapy water filled with floor polish, causing Toyoda to lose his balance and consequently let go of the nice Nurse Tyne.

Marlboro then grabbed the mop and pushed Toyoda out into the stairwell, forcing him to tumble down the metal and concrete stairs, rendering him unconscious and ending up with the *aisupikku* sticking in his thigh.

Chiharu Toyoda was taken from L.A. County Hospital to the prison hospital across town. Tanaka had him placed in the same room as Atsuki Ryujin. He had a blond-haired, blue-eyed Caucasian police officer who spoke fluent Japanese sitting outside their room, knowing they would converse in Japanese.

"Toyoda-san, is that you?" Ryujin asked.

"*Hai*. What happened to you?"

"I was foolish. I wanted to gain favor with the *oyabun*. I tried to kill the paint store owner but got snared in a booby trap and ended up losing my right foot. I should have listened to you. So, what has happened to you, Toyoda-san?"

"The oyabun sent me to rub out a police officer who had Kenji Yamamoto killed in prison. We had staged a car crash where he was severely burnt but did not die, so I was sent to finish the job, but I, too, have failed."

"Did the police injure you?"

"No. It was a hospital janitor who tricked me and caused me to impale myself with my *aisupikku*."

"That is most unfortunate."

"The odd thing is that I'm sure I had seen that janitor somewhere before."

"What did they arrest you for? Attempted murder?"

"No kidnapping of a nurse. You?"

"Breaking and entering and attempted murder."

"*Nanite Kokoda* (oh my God)!" Toyoda exclaimed.

"What?"

"I just remembered who that janitor is."

"Who?"

"Butch Baker, the paint store owner. The bastard has ruined my life."

"Mine, too. At least you have both your feet," Ryujin said as he began to cry.

"Marlboro! What the Hell are you doing here?" Tanaka asked.

"Wakabayashi twisted her ankle, so I brought her to the ER to see a doc."

"How did you know we were up here?"

"I saw the blue swarm, asked a friend, and decided to see if I could help."

"You're lucky it turned out the way it did. You coulda got somebody killed!"

"Coulda, woulda, shoulda."

"Why the mop and pail?"

"I figured you couldn't use your heaters because of the oxygen. So, I thought of trying the old mop and pail routine."

"The old mop and pail routine? Never heard of it."

"That's cause I just made it up," Marlboro grinned.

Tanaka shook his head in disbelief, "Marlboro, one of these days, you'll… Oh, fuck it. How's Wakabayashi?"

"I don't know. Let's go see."

They took the elevator down to the ER at about the time the uniforms were escorting Chiharu Toyoda into the prison hospital van. Wakabayashi was still waiting to be seen by the doctor; her foot was now swollen to the size of a grapefruit, a black and blue grapefruit.

"Aiko Sugimoto Baker." The ER nurse called.

"I'll see you both later. I got a suspect to interview," Tanaka said.

Marlboro gave a slight wave as he wheeled Wakabayashi to see the doctor.

Marlboro drove Wakabayashi home two hours later with a plaster ankle cast and a pair of wooden crutches. On the way home, Wakabayashi said, "So, tell me again, you carried a mop and bucket of greasy, soapy water up four flights of stairs, pretended to be a janitor, not knowing what to expect when you got there, and just by sheer luck managed to trip up the goon holding a nurse hostage, thereby pushing him down a flight of stairs, knocking him out and causing him to stick an icepick in his thigh."

"Well, when you put it like that, it does sound kind of ridiculous," Marlboro chuckled.

Chapter Twenty
The Gorilla and The Punk

"I don't fucking believe it! Both the *Gorira* (gorilla) and that punk kid, Atsuki Ryujin are in the prison hospital. How is this possible?" Kobayashi screamed.

Kazz Daguchi and Yuuma Hagihara sat silently across from the *oyabun* at the *chabudai,* drinking sake. They looked at each other, wanting the other to suggest a plan, but neither had the courage to speak. Finally, Kobayashi said, "Two things will happen this week. One is that Daguchi is going to die, and two, that paint pusher Baker and his whore will disappear.

Daguchi, I should have sent you to eliminate that pig Daguchi instead of that *dōke* (buffoon) Toyoda. Shackleford is currently at L.A. County Hospital in the burn unit; apparently, he's under the constant watch of the police, so it will be difficult to achieve. Just tell me what you need, and it shall be done."

"*Hai, oyabun,*" said Daguchi with a short bow.

"Hagihara, you shall devise a plan to eliminate Butch Baker and his *baishunpu* (whore). I want them dead by week's end, understand?"

"*Hai, oyabun,*" Hagihara said bowing.

"Now, both of you go!" Kobayashi growled.

Sato, the office lackey, entered the room once Kazz Daguchi and Yuuma Hagihara had left and said, "Kobayashi-san, you have a phone call. It's *Saikōshidō-sha* (the supreme leader)."

Kobayashi almost wet himself; this could not be good. *Saikōshidō-sha* (the supreme leader) of the Black Rain Yakuza International, Hiroshi Takahashi, calling from Tokyo was rarely a good thing.

"*Kon'nichiwa,* Takahashi-san," Kobayashi muttered.

"Kobayashi, I have been hearing a lot of distressing things about your organization; there's been infighting leading to murder and multiple arrests. A couple of your people were maimed, and some were killed in prison. And worst of all, your business is being undermined by a *gaijin*. What have you to say?" Takahashi demanded.

Kobayashi lied through his teeth, "I don't know where you're hearing this from. But none of that is true. Things here are right on target; our revenues are up. That so-called *gaijin* problem is taken care of, and as far as arrests are concerned, there hasn't been anything out of the ordinary."

"What about Aoi Yamaguchi? I hear he died by *seppuku*."

"Aoi Yamaguchi was a traitor. He was planning a coup. When he was discovered, he chose the *Bushidō* Code," Kobayashi explained.

"I am coming to Los Angeles to see for myself how things are proceeding. I will arrive next Monday. I expect everything to be as you say, or you too shall follow in the way of the *Bushidō* Code."

CLICK!

Kobayashi felt sick to his stomach, his world was falling apart, and it was all that fucking *gaijin's* fault. He had to die and soon.

"I'm here to see my client, Chiharu Toyoda. I'm his attorney, Kazz Daguchi." Daguchi said as he offered the police officer his "card."

The officer gave Daguchi the once over and then said, "Open the briefcase, please."

There was nothing noteworthy but a couple of legal pads, several ballpoint pens, and an open pack of Wrigley Spearmint Gum.

The officer picked up the pack of gum, took a piece, and asked, "Ya mind?"

Daguchi answered, "No."

"Okay, Chiharu Toyoda is up on two, room 215. The elevator is around the corner.

Daguchi closed up his briefcase and made his way to the elevators. When he reached room 215, Toyoda was asleep, and Atsuki Ryujin was reading the latest edition of a Tarzan Manga comic book. Ryujin saw movement in the corner of his eye and saw Kazz Daguchi, dressed in a three-piece suit carrying a briefcase, enter the room.

"Daguchi-san. What are you doing here?" Ryujin asked.

"I am here to speak to Chiharu. How are you doing? I have heard about your misfortune. I am so sorry."

"*Arigatō*, Daguchi-san."

Toyoda eventually awoke from hearing voices. He was surprised to see Kazz Daguchi standing next to his bed.

"Daguchi-san. What are you doing here? Are you here to bust us out?"

"No. That would be impossible. I told them that I was your lawyer. We don't have much time; I need you to tell me everything you can about the hospital setup where Shackleford is being kept."

"Why?"

"Kobayashi wants me to eliminate him before he can speak."

"It cannot be done, Daguchi-san. He is too heavily guarded."

"I must try."

"He is in the burn unit ward on the fourth floor. There is an armed policeman in his room. However, they can't use their guns because the rooms are filled with pure oxygen, which might work to your advantage."

"*Arigatō*, Toyoda-san. I wish you and Ryujin all the best. *Sayōnara*."

And with that, he was gone, leaving Toyoda and Ryujin to face their fates with no help from the Black Rain. It would probably be a long prison stretch for Toyoda, whereas young Atsuki Ryujin, having suffered the loss of his foot, might get sympathy from a jury.

Chiharu Toyoda would be transferred to the county jail to await trial in a few days, while Atsuki Ryujin would remain in the prison hospital for several months undergoing physical therapy.

After the attempt on Officer Rusty Shackleford's life, Detective Tanaka decided to move Shackleford to a different room, and he added another police officer to guard him. Knowing that firearms couldn't be used, both officers were issued billy clubs, brass knuckles, and saps. Sergeant Olden Foster had an eight-inch switchblade knife concealed in his knee-high sock. He began carrying the stiletto ever since his gun jammed and was almost killed in close combat with a couple of street toughs. He showed it to Officer Joseph Lopez, who was duly impressed.

"Holy shit, *jefe* (boss), that's one bitching pig sticker. I got to get me one of those. Where did you get that bad boy?" Lopez asked.

"I picked it up at the Cash & Dash Pawn Shop on Venice and Grand a couple of years ago," Foster said.

"I gotta have one, especially on this assignment. Will you be okay while I run out for a few minutes?"

"Just be quick about it. It'll be my ass in a sling if something happens and you're not around."

"Thanks, *esse* (homie)," Lopez said as he ran towards the stairs.

As Kazz Daguchi sat in the County Hospital parking lot devising his plan, he saw Officer Lopez running towards the squad car and then driving off.

Daguchi figured now would be the time to strike. Armed with a *tantō* and half a dozen *shuriken* (throwing stars), he planned to waltz into the main entrance casually, purchase a bouquet of flowers, ride the elevator up to the fourth floor, and attack the guard, kill him if necessary, and then eliminate Police Officer Rusty Shackleford.

Unlike Chiharu Toyoda, Daguchi was dressed in a three-piece suit and dark green aviator sunglasses to conceal the fact that he was Japanese. He first walked towards the room where Toyoda said Shackleford was, but when he got there, the room was vacant. He proceeded to slowly stroll down the halls, looking to see if he could see a policeman; it wasn't until he had almost made a complete circle that he spotted the officer sitting in a room reading a copy of the L.A. Times.

Daguchi reached into his pocket, removed one of the shuriken, and, with a forceful flick of his wrist, fired off the throwing star, piercing the L.A. Times and striking Sergeant Olden Foster in the chest. Lucky for him, he had the foresight to be wearing a bulletproof vest. As Foster reached for his truncheon, Daguchi pulled the *tantō* out, hidden in the bouquet of flowers, and began to charge.

Foster was able to fend off the initial attack from Daguchi's jabbing and thrusting with the *tantō* with the billy club, but he knew he was up against a superior adversary. It didn't take long for Daguchi to inflect several deep cuts on Foster's arms and thighs. Kazz Daguchi, the ultimate assassin, was moving in for the kill when he felt a sharp pain in the middle of his back; as he instinctively reached behind his back to see what was the source of the pain, Police Sergeant Olden Foster took the opportunity to deliver a crushing line drive to Daguchi's head, felling him like a giant redwood. The sound of Foster's truncheon cracking Daguchi's skull was so loud that it was heard down at the nurse's station on the third floor. It was later revealed that the source of Daguchi's back pain was Officer Lopez's newly purchased eight-inch switchblade knife.

Kazz Daguchi was treated for a cracked skull, concussion, and a stab wound in the back. Then, he was sent to the prison hospital, where he was admitted into the room next to Chiharu Toyoda and Atsuki Ryujin.

What Daguchi, Toyoda, Ryujin, and Kobayashi didn't know was that shortly after Daguchi's attack, Police Officer Rusty Shackleford, a veteran of eighteen years on the LAPD, passed away from his injuries, having never gained consciousness. It wasn't until three days later that his obituary appeared in the local newspapers when Kobayashi freaked out at the loss of his two top lieutenants.

"*Kuso ttare* (God damnit)!" Kobayashi thundered.

Marlboro had just finished repairing the basement window that Atsuki Ryujin had snuck into and resetting the scraggy tread on the staircase leading up to the paint store. He re-greased the top six treads with STP 30-weight motor oil and bolted the basement door shut.

"Oh, John, could you come upstairs when you're done?" Wakabayashi called out.

"Be right there," Marlboro answered, climbing the stairs up to the apartment.

She wasn't there when he got to the landing that led to the living room. He walked into the kitchen, but there was no Wakabayashi. He peeked into the bathroom; again, there was no Wakabayashi. Ultimately, he called out, "Wakabayashi, where are you?"

"I'm in the bookcase," She cooed.

He swung open the door leading to the safe space where they sleep at night to find her lying naked on the small mat with nothing but the plaster cast on her ankle and a smile on her face.

"My cast itches. Can you come and scratch it for me?" She said, spreading her legs.

Marlboro laid down beside her and began kissing her. He started kissing her on the lips and slowly began moving down to her breasts and stomach, and finally, he buried his face in her *chitsu* as she moaned with delight. He, too, got naked and then mounted her from behind, as it was excruciating for her to keep her leg raised during missionary sex.

Afterward, they lay in a throng of exhaustion, sweaty, breathing deeply, snuggled together, eventually falling asleep. They didn't wake up until the following day when the phone rang.

"Hello, *Natsukashī Kokoro* Paints," Marlboro said.

"Marlboro, this is Tanaka. Did I wake you?"

"No! We've been up for hours. What's up?"

"I need you to be at the courthouse today at eleven."

"How come?"

"Atsuki Ryujin is being arraigned on B&E and attempted murder."

"We'll be there, man."

"I don't need Hana to be there, just you."

"Well, with all the shit going down, I don't want to leave her here by herself."

"Okay, I understand. See you both at eleven. Room 333. Bye."

"*Sayōnara*," Marlboro said.

Wakabayashi asked, "Tanaka?"

"Yeah, he needs us to attend Ryujin's arraignment. We have to be there at eleven."

"You know what, Marlboro?"

"What?"

"My ankle is itching again. Do you think you could scratch my itch again?"

"I'm here to serve, doll."

Makoto Shinazugawa, one of Kobayashi's primary enforcers, extortion collectors, and bone-breaker, was shaking down Fuji Yamamoto, the owner of Yamamoto-san to musk-tachi (Yamamoto and Sons) Grocery Store when Marlboro and Wakabayashi walked in.

"Good afternoon, Yamamoto-san," Marlboro said.

"Good afternoon, Mr. Baker, Mrs. Baker."

Shinazugawa, holding a Louisville Slugger baseball bat, gave Marlboro the stink-eye and growled, "Go on about your business, *gaijin*!"

Marlboro glanced at Yamamoto, who had a trickle of blood flowing from his nose.

"Are you all right, Mr. Yamamoto?" Wakabayashi asked.

"Yeah, he's fine. Just a little nosebleed. Ain't that right?" Shinazugawa asked as he glared at the old shop owner.

"*Hai*. Just a little nosebleed."

Marlboro and Wakabayashi walked down a couple of aisles and turned around to peek to see what was going on. Shinazugawa waited until the *gaijin* and his whore had disappeared, then he grabbed the old shopkeeper by the arm and began to twist it behind the old man's back.

"Listen, *rōjin* (old man), you're already two weeks behind in paying your protection money, so if you don't want this arm broken in two places, I suggest you get me that money by closing time tonight, or else!" Shinazugawa snarled while thumping the bat on Yamamoto's head.

Marlboro and Wakabayashi stepped out from the aisle, and Marlboro said, "Strike one."

"Back off, *Gesu yarō* (asshole)."

"You play baseball, dipshit?" Marlboro asked.

Shinazugawa let the old man's arm go and turned his attention to Marlboro. "How would you like to find out?" Shinazugawa said as he took a big swing at Marlboro's head, who ducked, causing Shinazugawa to miss.

"A swing and a miss for strike two," Wakabayashi said, holding up two fingers.

Shinazugawa's face grew red, and as he was getting ready to take another swipe at Marlboro, Wakabayashi did a flying roundabout kick to the big man's chin, knocking him out cold.

Marlboro looked at the store owner and asked, "Which hand did he hit you with?"

"*Kare no migite* (his right hand)."

Marlboro placed Shinazugawa's right hand on the checkout counter, and when He regained consciousness, he took the Louisville Slugger and smacked the bat down on his hand as hard as he could. There was the sickening sound of bones breaking, followed by the screams of pain.

KRUUUNNCHHH! EEEYYYAAAHHH!!

"Strike three. You're out!" Marlboro said, giving the umpire's thumb gesture.

"You're a dead man, *gaijin*!" Shinazugawa whimpered, holding his shattered hand.

"If I see your ugly puss harassing any of the other merchants, next time it'll be your head; I'll be bashing, not your hand. Ya dig? Now scram!"

Chapter Twenty-One
145 MPH

"All rise. The Honorable William F. Russell is now presiding—criminal cause for arraignment, Docket Number 24-CR-574, the State of California versus Atsuki Ryujin.

Counsel, please state your appearances for the record and spell your names for the reporter, including the pretrial officer." said the courtroom deputy.

"Good afternoon, Your Honor. Alex Norris, A-L-E-X, N-O-R-R-I-S; for the Government.

"Good afternoon. You may be seated and remain seated throughout the remainder of the hearing. Thank you." Judge Russell said.

"Good afternoon, Your Honor. For Mr. Ryujin, R-Y-U-J-I-N; Richard Piastri, P-I-A-S-T-R-I, who is present to my right, Your Honor." Said Richard Piastri, the attorney for Atsuki Ryujin.

"Now, Mr. Ryujin, I am going to begin by asking you a few questions about your background. Would you please state your full name," Judge Russell said.

"Atsuki Ryujin."

"Please speak right into that microphone that is in front of you. Mr. Ryujin. Thank you. And do you go by any other names, sir?

"No."

"What is your birthday; how old are you?"

"I'm twenty-four."

"Are you a citizen of the United States?"

"Yes, sir."

"What kind of work do you do, Mr. Ryujin?"

"I am the assistant to the regional manager for Takahashi Industries."

"And what exactly is Takahashi Industries?"

"They are an import and export company."

"What sort of things do they import and export?"

"All kinds of things. Electronics, food items, clothing, nothing in particular and everything in general."

"Now, sir, have you taken any drugs, consumed any medicine, taken any pills, or consumed any alcohol in the past 24 hours?"

"Yes, sir."

"What have you taken?"

"Your Honor, my client is currently residing in the prison hospital because he has recently had his right foot amputated. He has been prescribed low doses of morphine for pain, as well as numerous antibiotics," Richard Piastri, his attorney, explained.

"Thank you, counselor. Mr. Ryujin, do you understand what is happening here today?" Russell asked.

"To some extent, yes."

"Defense Counsel, do you have any doubt as to your client's competence to proceed at this time?"

"No, Your Honor."

"Mr. Norris, do you have any doubt as to the defendant's competence to proceed at this time?"

"No, Your Honor," Norris replied.

"The Court hereby finds, based on the defendant's representations and the representations of all counsel of record, that the defendant is competent to proceed.

Now, Mr. Ryujin, it is essential for you to understand these proceedings. If, for any reason, you do not understand something that is being said to you, please raise your hand, and I will repeat and restate whatever it is you do not understand. Do you understand, sir?"

"Yes, Your Honor."

"Now, sir, you have the right to remain silent. If you start to make a statement, you may stop anytime. Any statements that you make to anyone other than your attorney may be used against you. Mr. Ryujin, do you understand that you have the right to counsel and the right to remain silent?"

"Yes, sir."

"Now, Mr. Ryujin, you are here today because a grand jury has returned an indictment, which was filed on June 9th of 1954, charging you with the following offenses: Count 1, First Degree Burglary into the *Natsukashī Kokoro* Paint Store in violation of Title 18, California State Penal Code, Section 459, *et sequentia*; Count 2, Attempted Murder California State Penal Code, § 664/187(a) PC *et sequentia*.

Mr. Ryujin, have you seen the indictment filed against you in this case?"

"Yes, I did."

"Have you had an opportunity to review that indictment with your attorney?"

"Yes."

"Do you understand the charges that are being made against you today, sir?"

"Yes."

"Mr. Ryujin, are you ready to plead, sir?"

"Yes, sir."

"What is your plea to Count 1 of the indictment, guilty or not guilty?"

"Not guilty."

"What is your plea to Count 2 of the indictment, guilty or not guilty?"

"Not guilty."

Judge Russell looked to the prosecution and asked,

"Mr. Norris, what is the Government's position on the question of detention or bail as to Mr. Ryujin?"

"Your Honor, the Government believes that Mr. Ryujin should be remanded to the prison hospital because he is still under the care of the prison doctor, and we feel that Mr. Ryujin constitutes a flight risk."

"All right. I am going to enter an order of detention pending trial. Defense Counsel, is there anything further you wish to say to the Court today at this time?" Russell asked.

Defense counsel Piastri said, "No, Judge. Thank you."

"Thank you."

"Mr. Prosecutor, is there anything further you wish to say to the Court at this time?"

"No. Your Honor."

"Thank you. Then we are adjourned."

The defendant, Atsuki Ryujin, handcuffed to his wheelchair, was taken back to the prison hospital; he passed seated in the gallery Detective Tanaka, Marlboro, and Wakabayashi.

Ryujin gave them the finger and shouted, *Rokudenashi* (bastards)!"

Marlboro smiled, waved, and said, "*Yoiichinichiwo* (have a nice day)."

Yuuma Hagihara, the ninja master, and *Kensei* (sword saint) reported to *Oyabun* Kobayashi to review his plans to attack the *Natsukashī Kokoro* Paint Store.

"I have conceived a plan that I believe will eliminate Butch Baker once and for all. We will strike the building from the basement, fire escape, front door, and the roof simultaneously."

Kobayashi asked, "What about the basement? Ryujin tried it, and he lost his foot. How is someone going to overcome that booby trap?"

"Steel bottom boots," Hagihara replied.

"Clever. The front door is solid metal."

"We will rip the door off its hinges with a wench hooked up to two tow trucks. We should be able to tear it right off, no problem."

"As far as attacking from the roof. We will scale down on ropes from the rooms of the Mikado Hotel and cut our way into the apartment with axes, and finally, we'll send men up the fire escape to enter the apartment through the windows."

"Be careful, we've lost half a dozen men going in through those windows," Kobayashi warned.

"I know; we've adapted some techniques to counter whatever Mr. Baker can throw at us."

"We have to take care of the *gaijin* no later than Saturday," Kobayashi said.

"Then Saturday it is."

"How many men do we have?"

"Twenty-four."

"Will that be enough?" Kobayashi asked.

"Should be more than enough. After all, it's just Baker and his crippled whore."

"Very good. So, in two days, I will finally be rid of that *gaichū* (vermin) Butch Baker. This calls for a toast," Kobayashi said, pouring two glasses of sake.

"*Kanpai* (cheers)!"

"*Kanpai*!"

Two county sheriff deputies arrived at the prison hospital early one morning with a writ to transfer Kazz Daguchi to the Los Angeles County Jail. The prison doctor had signed off on him being healthy enough to be released.

Unbeknownst to the staff, Daguchi had hidden a metal fork from dinner the night before and had concealed it in between his butt cheeks, believing that no one would consider looking there for a weapon, and he was right.

When the deputies came to take him away, while they were unlocking his handcuff from the metal sidebar of his hospital bed, Daguchi retrieved the metal fork from his butt and overcame one of the sheriff's deputies, shoved the metal fork up against his jugular and relieved him of his revolver. Now, holding both officers at gunpoint, he made them undress, wearing one of the uniforms he stole the other, and made his getaway in their squad car, leaving both deputies wearing only their underwear, mouths taped, and handcuffed to the hospital bed next to Atsuki Ryujin.

Daguchi drove from the prison hospital to Kobayashi's headquarters in Little Tokyo with the siren blaring and the lights flashing. The joint emptied out like rats from a sinking ship when he arrived. Nobody recognized Daguchi in a copper's uniform; he strolled right into the conference room with no one challenging him. Even Kobayashi didn't recognize him until he removed his aviator sunglasses and sheriff's hat.

"Hi, boss," Daguchi said with a shit-eating grin.

Kobayashi looked the escaped prisoner up and down in a sheriff's uniform and laughed hysterically.

"Daguchi, what the fuck have you done?"

"I issued myself a jackrabbit parole."

"And from the sound of the siren, I assume that you carjacked a police car, as well."

"Actually, it's a Sheriff's patrol car."

"What do you plan on doing with it, Daguchi? You know you can't keep it."

"I thought I could sell it for parts."

"Well, you better do it quick. I'm sure there's an APB out for the car and for you. Where are you going to stay now that you're a fugitive?" Kobayashi asked.

"I thought I could stay here and help get rid of that *gaijin*."

Kobayashi thought it over for several minutes before answering, "Okay. But you get a room at the Mikado and don't show your face until I give you permission. You dig? Now go and get rid of that squad car!"

Daguchi returned to the squad car and sped off with the siren blaring and the flashing lights on. He was headed for the 405 Freeway North when an LAPD motorcycle cop spotted him. The high-speed pursuit began when Daguchi entered the 405 from the Santa Monica onramp at 110 mph.

By the time Daguchi reached the Ventura Boulevard exit, he had six LAPD and four L.A. County Sheriff's cars on his tail, weaving in and out of Tuesday morning rush hour traffic. When he passed the Roscoe Boulevard exit, the number of police and sheriff's cars had doubled. Speeds were now exceeding 130 mph. Above in the sky, Daguchi and his entourage were trailed by two police choppers and a News 5 helicopter broadcasting the chase live on TV.

It was fast approaching the time for Daguchi to make a decision. Was he willing to surrender and spend decades in prison or go out in a blaze of glory? The stuff that legends are made of. He chose the latter. Once that was decided, it came down to whether to snuff it with a shootout or a go out in a 140-mile-an-hour blaze of glory car crash. Both had their advantages, and both had drawbacks. He couldn't seem to make up his mind, so he decided to let fate make the choice for him.

He was fast approaching the 101 Freeway heading west. He took the exit ramp at over 85 miles per hour; he couldn't believe he managed to keep the car on the road at that speed. When he glanced in the rear-view mirror, he saw two patrol cars skid off the ramp and collide with each other.

Daguchi's patrol car was screaming down the 101, heading towards the Topanga Canyon Boulevard exit. He waited until the very last second before veering off the 101 and onto Topanga Canyon Boulevard. He slammed on the brakes hard and made a murderous left turn, nearly missing a large yellow school bus filled with kids; as he passed the bus, he could see the terrified faces of the twenty-four sixth graders looking back at him. At least nine kids wet themselves, and one shit his pants.

Topanga Canyon Boulevard is a series of twisty right and left turns that would give Formula One drivers a thrill traveling at the speeds Daguchi was achieving. For over twenty miles, Daguchi didn't put a foot wrong all the way to where Topanga Canyon Boulevard T-bones into Pacific Coast Highway. When he headed north toward Malibu, he heard on the police scanner in the patrol car that the Sheriff's Department had set up a roadblock just south of the Malibu Pier. They had placed four Caterpillar bulldozers side by side across the highway, flanked on both sides of the road were two Malibu police squad cars. He would either have to stop and surrender or…

As he approached the roadblock, Daguchi slammed his foot down onto the accelerator and screamed, *"Banzi!"*

BAAROOOOM!

That evening, an LAPD police spokesperson made a statement on Channel 5 KTLA News. *"At two-forty-five this afternoon, Mr. Kazz Daguchi, an escaped prisoner from the Los Angeles Prison Hospital, died in a fiery crash on the Pacific Coast Highway after a fifty-five-minute high-speed chase from Westwood down to Malibu where, at times, he was clocked doing over 145 miles-per-hour into a roadblock of four Caterpillar bulldozers. Death was instantaneous. There is no known reason why Mr. Kazz Daguchi refused to surrender to authorities. There is a video of this tragic event; viewer discretion is advised. No police or civilians were injured. Mr. Kazz Daguchi was a member of the Los Angeles chapter of the Japanese yakuza known as the Black Rain, which deals in extorsion, drugs, prostitution, and loan sharking. The LAPD, LA County Sheriff's Office, and the District Attorney's office continue investigating the incident. Thank you."*

When the phone rang, Marlboro and Wakabayashi had just finished watching the news story about Kazz Daguchi's high-speed chase and scorching demise on Channel 5.

"*Natsukashī Kokoro* paints, can I help you?" Marlboro said.

"Marlboro, Tanaka. Have you seen the news?"

"Yeah, we just saw it on Channel 5. That's the guy I knocked down the stairs who tried to whack Shackleford. How did he escape?"

"Apparently, he overpowered two sheriff's deputies, took their uniforms, and stole their squad cars. We know he stopped off to see his boss, Kobayashi, through the tracking devices installed on all LAPD and sheriff's cars. Then the dumb son of a bitch fired up the siren and the berries and cherries (police car lights) as he headed towards the freeway. It's almost like he wanted to get caught," Tanaka said.

"Well, obviously, he didn't. He was already caught. I think he figured once the cops spotted him, he had three choices: give up and spend years in the slammer, die in a shootout, or wham, bam, now you're spam."

"Yes, very poetic. Well, I just wondered if you had seen it. I guess it means you'll have one less yakuza to deal with."

"They keep thinning the herd. Thanks, detective. Talk soon."

CLICK

Across Little Tokyo, Kio Kobayashi was sitting down to dinner when the phone rang.

"*Moshi moshi* (hello)?"

"Kobayashi-san, there is something that you must see. Turn on Channel 5 now," Yuuma Hagihara said.

"What is it?"

"It's Daguchi, *oyabun*. There is a story on channel five news."

Kobayashi walked over to the TV set in his living room, switched it on, and sat mesmerized at what he saw. Aerial footage of Daguchi involved in a high-speed car chase ending in his apparent suicidal crash into several bulldozers, resulting in death.

After seeing the news footage and listening to the police spokesperson, Kobayashi returned to the phone and said, "I have never seen such bravery since my father flew his Mitsubishi Zero into and sank the USS Saint Lo carrier. Daguchi was truly a kamikaze. I will say a *norito* for him. He will be honored."

Chapter Twenty-Two
Supreme Leader

Hiroshi Takahashi, *Saikōshidō-sha* (supreme leader) of the Black Rain Yakuza International, had been receiving weekly reports from Hanzō Doumekii, the *oyabun* of the San Francisco Black Rain chapter. Doumekii had a long-running feud with Kio Kobayashi, the *oyabun* of Little Tokyo's chapter of the Black Rain; each had been trying to undermine the other's authority to gain control of each other's territory.

It would now appear that Doumekii had the upper hand as Little Tokyo's chapter of the Black Rain was going through a severe rough patch thanks to John Marlboro and Officer Hana Wakabayashi. Kobayashi lost fourteen soldiers and lieutenants who were either killed or wounded in "action."

"*Saikōshidō-sha*, I think it my duty to inform you of another catastrophic event that brought dishonor to Kobayashi and the Black Rain," Doumekii said with glee.

"And what exactly would that be, Doumekii?"

"One of Kobayashi's lieutenants, Kazz Daguchi, was involved in a high-speed car chase and was killed when he drove head-on into several construction heavy equipment machines, bringing a spotlight onto the organization. I think it shows a lack of control over his men."

"I have heard that one of your men made a foolish attempt on the paint shop owner, hence losing his foot. Is that not correct, Doumekii-san?" Takahashi asked.

"*Hai*. But Atsuki Ryujin was under the command of Kobayashi."

"True. But aren't you the one who sent the young, inexperienced Ryujin down to Little Tokyo? I believe that Kobayashi had asked that you send some of your top men to assist him for a sizeable percentage of his revenue, yet you chose to send unprepared, incompetent, and untested men in hopes of seeing him fail. Is that not right, Doumekii?"

"*Saikōshidō-sha*, I don't think it was reasonable that I should have sent down my very best soldiers. I mean, how hard could it be to rid oneself of a simple paint shop owner? I believe that I could rid the pest myself."

"Then do so," Takahashi said.

"What?" A flummoxed Doumekii asked.

"I will let Kobayashi know you will be there tomorrow to rid him of his problem. And if you are successful, there will be a bonus for you. *Kōun o* (good luck)."

"But. But..."

CLICK

When Kobayashi got word that his nemesis Doumekii was coming down by order of the *Saikōshidō-sha* to try and kill Butch Baker, a feat that none of his men could accomplish, he burst out in laughter. Finally, he would be rid of this scourge once and for all. He wondered what he had done to deserve such a blessing from the *Saikōshidō-sha*.

If all goes well and Baker liberates him of his adversary, he must give the *Saikōshidō-sha* something special when he arrives Monday. Maybe Doumekii's head on a platter.

Doumekii's plan was simple: walk into the paint store, pull out his Walther PPK pistol, shoot Baker, and walk out. No muss, no fuss. Unfortunately, sometimes simple isn't so simple. As Doumekii would soon discover.

He was personally picked up at Los Angeles International Airport by Kobayashi. Doumekii had no luggage, no briefcase, just his pistol tucked inside his shoulder holster.

"*Ohayō* (good morning), Doumekii-san," Kobayashi said with a slight bow of the head.

"*Ohayō* (good morning), Kobayashi -san," Doumekii said, returning the greeting with a slight head bow.

Neither one meant it; they both wanted the other one dead. As they were being driven from the airport to Little Tokyo, they engaged in polite small talk.

When they arrived, Doumekii said, "Just drop me in front of the paint store and keep the engine running; I'll be right out."

Kobayashi smiled, "*Hai*. Be careful."

Doumekii got out of the black Lincoln, rang the doorbell, and walked in. Moments later, three gunshots rang out.

POW. POW. POW.

Doumekii opened the door, took two steps, and collapsed on the sidewalk face down, dead, with two gunshots in his stomach.

"I told him to be careful. Kyō, take me back to the office," Kobayashi calmly told his driver.

Within minutes, Detective Tanaka and two black and whites pulled up in front of *Natsukashī Kokoro*.

Tanaka rolled the body over, looked at the uniforms, and asked, "Does anybody recognize this mutt?"

No one raised their hand, so Tanaka entered the paint store where Marlboro and Wakabayashi were waiting.

"So, Mr. Baker, what the Hell happened?"

"Well, Detective Tanaka, I'm stacking paint cans over there in the corner when this goombah waltzes in and asks me if I'm Butch Baker. I no sooner say that's me when he pulls out a gat and fires one off. Pow."

"Then what happened?" Tanaka asked.

"Lucky for us, we were wearing our bulletproof vest because the dumb jamoke popped me right in the chest, knocking me down. Aiko pulled out her roscoe and fired off two rounds, hitting the hatchet man in the breadbasket. He almost fitted me for a wooden kimono, the bastard."

"Wooden kimono?" Tanaka asked.

"Yeah, you know, a coffin," Marlboro said.

"Gee, I hadn't heard that one before."

"You really need to get out more, Detective Tanaka."

"Well, I'm going to need you and Mrs. Baker to come down to the station and give us a full statement."

"Let's go and get it over with," Marlboro said.

As they were locking up, one of the uniformed officers who had responded to several of the previous shootings said, "Mr. Baker, this is my fourth time out here; it seems to me like somebody really got it in for you."

"Ya think."

"*Saikōshidō-sha*, it's Kio Kobayashi; I am calling to regretfully inform you that Hanzō Doumekii was shot dead this morning in an altercation with the owner of the *Natsukashī Kokoro* paint store. I tried to warn him that the owner was no pushover and to be careful, but he paid me no mind."

"Kobayashi-san, I must meet this worthy opponent before you eliminate him, so I will be coming to Los Angeles tomorrow. There are so few men that have garnered my respect, such as this Butch Baker. I look forward to meeting him. After he is dead, we will have much to speak of. I will see you tomorrow."

CLICK

"May I have your attention? Announcing the arrival of Japanese Airlines flight thirty-six at gate twenty-one."

As the passengers began to disembark, Kio Kobayashi stood patiently waiting, hat in hand, straining to see the *Saikōshidō-sha*, Hiroshi Takahashi. After half a dozen people exited the plane, he saw Takahashi's bald head bobbing up and down as he walked up the exit ramp toward the gate.

Once Takahashi stepped into the lounge area, Kobayashi bowed deeply and said, "*Rosanzerusu e yōkoso* (welcome to Los Angeles) Takahashi-san."

"*Arigatō*, Kobayashi-san," Takahashi said with a half bow.

"Please follow me. I have my car waiting. Do you have any luggage?" Kobayashi asked.

"*Hai*, two suitcases."

"I have my driver waiting at the baggage claim," Kobayashi said as he led his master through the terminal.

When they reached the luggage carousel, Kyo, Kobayashi's driver, had procured Takahashi's two alligator suitcases and patiently waited. Once he saw Kobayashi and Takahashi, he picked up the suitcases and led them out of the *terminal* to the black Lincoln stretch limo sitting at the curb.

After Kyo placed the suitcases in the trunk, he headed up Century Boulevard toward the 405 Freeway.

"Would you like to stop at the Beverly Hills Hotel first so you might freshen up, Takahashi-san?"

"No. I want to go to the *Natsukashī Kokoro* and see this *gaijin* Butch Baker and his *tsuma* (wife). Is it true that she is the one who shot and killed Hanzō Doumekii?"

"*Hai*, Takahashi-san."

"Interesting."

"Kyo, take us to *Natsukashī Kokoro*," Kobayashi said.

"*Kashikomarimashita* (yes sir)."

When they arrived at the paint store, Marlboro was about to put the "out to lunch" sign in the window when he spotted Kobayashi and an older Japanese man, nattily dressed and business-looking, walking hurriedly toward the store.

"Ah, Mr. Kobayashi, it's a pleasure to see you again. I was getting ready to close the shop for lunch. But, for you," Marlboro said, gesturing for them to come in.

"*Arigatō*, Butch," Kobayashi said.

"Is there something I can do for you?"

"My *Saikōshidō-sha*, Mr. Takahashi, wanted to meet you," Kobayashi said.

"Well, it's a pleasure to meet you, Mr. Takahashi."

"Mr. Baker, I have heard so much about you from Kobayashi-san that I just had to come by and see the man who has given my organization so much trouble."

"Your organization?" Marlboro asked, playing dumb.

"Come. Come, Mr. Baker. You know perfectly well that I am speaking of the Black Rain. You have been a torn in my side for long enough. You must know that this cannot and will not continue," Takahashi warned.

"Oh, so the Black Rain is closing shop and leaving Little Tokyo? Nothing personal, Mr. Takahashi, but I don't think you'll be missed."

"Very funny, Mr. Baker."

"Please, call me Butch," Marlboro said with a grin.

Wakabayashi came hobbling down the stairs and said, "Butch, do we have company?"

"Yes, dear. You remember Mr. Kobayashi. And this here is his boss, Mr. Takahashi. Gentlemen, my wife, Aiko."

Wakabayashi walked over, using her crutches, where the three of them were talking. She held out her hand and said, "So, good to see you again, Mr. Kobayashi. And it is a pleasure to meet you, Mr. Takahashi."

Takahashi bowed and asked, "Mrs. Baker, is it true that you shot Hanzō Doumekii yesterday?"

"*Hai*. That's right. This isn't Tombstone or Dodge City; this isn't the Wild West; we can't have somebody just come in here, start waving a gun around, and take a shot at me or my husband and get away with it. He shot at Butch, so I shot him. Twice."

"My compliments, Mrs. Baker, Hanzō Doumekii was quite handy with a gun. He must have been dazzled by your beauty," Takahashi said.

"Dear, Mr. Takahashi was just explaining that the Black Rain is leaving Little Tokyo. Isn't that right, Mr. Takahashi?" Marlboro asked.

"Very humorous, Butch. No, it is you who will be leaving Little Tokyo sooner than you might think. You will be leaving either alive or dead."

"Well, that's rather rude," Marlboro said with a smirk.

"Was that a treat, Mr. Takahashi?" Wakabayashi asked.

"No, Mrs. Baker, it was a promise."

"Well, we look forward to it, Mr. Takahashi. Will you and Mr. Kobayashi be leading the charge? No? I didn't think so," Marlboro said.

"Good day, Butch. Mrs. Baker. Enjoy your lunch." Takahashi sniggered.

"*Sayōnara*, ya'll come back, now. Ya hear," Marlboro said with a phony southern accent.

Chapter Twenty-Three
The Duke

"Detective Tanaka speaking."

"Yuki, Marlboro here. We just had a visit from Kobayashi and some big muckety-muck named Takahashi."

"What did they want?"

"I got the sense that Takahashi was the big cheese, the head honcho, the grand fromage. "

"I got it. The top dog."

"And he wanted to check out the paint store and size up Wakabayashi and me. I got the feeling that a full-scale assault is imminent. Probably either tonight or tomorrow night." Marlboro said.

"Are you and Wakabayashi ready?"

"Oh, I think we are more than ready. So far, I am not impressed with these clowns. However, they may have saved their best hatchet men for the big dance. But if we start to get overwhelmed, I'll be sure to give you a call," Marlboro said.

"Is there anything that you need from me?"

"Yeah, could you pick up an order that I'm going to call into The Original Pantry Café and deliver it?"

"You're joking me, right?"

"No! I've been eating nothing but fish heads and tofu for the past month, and if I'm going to go down fighting, I need some good old US of A diner chow. So, could you do a fella a solid?"

"Okay. Go ahead and call it in. I'm on my way to The Original Pantry Café. See ya in a bit." Tanaka said.

CLICK

"The Original Pantry Café."

"Yeah, this is John Marlboro. I need to place an order for pick up," Marlboro said.

"Oh, hey Johnny, it's Peggy. I haven't seen you around. Where have you been keeping yourself? Is everything okay?"

"Everything is Jake, doll, and you?"

"Oh, you know, same old, same old. What can I get ya?"

"I'd like a bowl of beef stew with a salad."

Peggy shouted out to the cook, "*One Bossy in a bowl with a side of cow feed.*"

"A hamburger, rare with onions."

"*One on the hoof. Make it Cry.*"

"And a hotdog with sauerkraut."

"*Gimme a bloodhound in the hay.* Is that it?"

"Yeah, doll. A Detective Tanaka is swinging by to pick it up shortly."

"Okay, Johnny, you take care, and I hope to see you soon," She said.

"That makes two of us. See ya, doll."

CLICK

Kobayashi and Takahashi were having drinks in the Polo Lounge at the Beverly Hills Hotel. Kobayashi was drinking a gin and tonic, and Takahashi had a Tom Collins while splitting an order of 290-dollar Imperial Osetra Caviar. Takahashi was inquiring about Kobayashi's plans on how he was planning to get rid of the arrogant *gaijin* when he noticed the American film star John Wayne sauntering into the bar and sat next to Kobayashi.

Takahashi leaned over Kobayashi and said, "Excuse me, are you perhaps John Wayne?"

"That's right, pilgrim."

"I am your biggest fan. May I buy you a drink? It would be a great honor, Mr. Wayne."

"Why, that's mighty neighborly of you, pilgrim."

The bartender came up to the Duke and asked, "What can I get you, Mr. Wayne?"

"Whiskey, and don't skimp on the hooch."

"Yes, sir."

Once Wayne got his drink, he held up his glass of whiskey and said, "Here's mud in your eye."

He tilted the glass back and swallowed the whole drink in one gulp.

"Another, Mr. Wayne?" Kobayashi asked.

"If you're buying."

The bartender brought Wayne another. The Duke asked, "Where are you boys from?"

Kobayashi said, "I'm from Los Angeles, and Mr. Takahashi is visiting from Tokyo, Japan."

"Japan, huh?"

"*Hai*," Takahashi said with a toothy grin.

"You know, did either of you fellas ever see Sands of Iwo Jima or Flying Leatherneck?"

"Yes, both very powerful," Takahashi answered.

Wayne downed the second whiskey, turned to Takahashi, and held up his empty glass, expecting him to offer another round.

Takahashi obliged, buying the Duke whiskey number three. By now, Wayne was getting slightly inebriated when he said, "Yeah, I killed a lot of you little monkeys in both of those, you know."

"Yeah," Kobayashi said.

"You know?"

"Yeah."

"You know?"

"Yeah, little monkeys," Takahashi said.

"Your darn tooting, Back then, we were making movies showing us killing a bunch of you Japs and Nazis and winning the war. Now, we're duking it out against those fucking Commies, you know?"

"Yeah," Kobayashi said.

"You know?"

"Yeah."

"You know?"

"Yeah, fucking Commies," Takahashi said.

"Damn straight, pilgrim!" The Duke said as he slammed his empty glass on the bar.

He stood up off of the barstool, put his arms around both Kobayashi and Takahashi, looked around the polo lounge, and whispered, "You know, fellas, I bet there's a whole lot of Commies sitting right here in this here bar. And my good friend "Tail Gunner Joe" Joseph McCarthy will ferret them Commie bastards outta Hollywood. I tell you what. Well, boys, I got to meet up with my good friend John Ford. We're going to be shooting a film in Ireland with that fiery redhead Maureen O'Hara. Thanks for the drinks, pilgrims."

Watching John Wayne walk away, Takahashi held up his Tom Collins and said, "*Kōshaku e* (to the Duke).

Kobayashi emptied his gin and tonic, slammed down his glass *ala* John Wayne, and said, "*Kōshaku e*."

The two sat silently at the bar, basking in the afterglow of rubbing elbows with the Duke. The bartender broke the mood when he asked if they would like another drink.

"*Hai*," Kobayashi said.

Once the drinks were delivered, Takahashi asked, "So, what is the plan for our friends, the Bakers?"

Kobayashi looked around to ensure no one was eavesdropping before speaking, "Yuuma Hagihara, my ninja master, has devised an ingenious plan. We will strike the building from the basement, fire escape, front door, and roof simultaneously. Tomorrow at midnight, we will rip the metal front door off its hinges with a wench hooked up to two tow trucks where ten men will enter. Simultaneously, six men will scale down on ropes from the rooms at the Mikado Hotel and cut their way into the apartment below with axes, two men will enter the basement through the window, and finally, we'll send eight men to climb up the fire escape to enter the apartment through the windows."

"How many men do you have?" Takahashi asked.

"Twenty-four. I've told them to show no mercy."

"I want their heads delivered to me, understand?"

"Yeah," Kobayashi said.

"Understand?"

"Yeah."

"Understand?"

"Yeah, heads delivered," Kobayashi said.

"Damn straight, pilgrim!" Takahashi said with a grin.

Kobayashi and Takahashi weren't the only ones basking in the afterglow, but for Marlboro and Wakabayashi, it wasn't because of sucking up to the Duke that got them off; it was good old fashion sex. They lay exhausted in a sweaty, entangled embrace, breathing deeply with the cocoon of the false bookcase, knowing that sometime soon, they would be attacked and possibly killed. As Marlboro philosophically put it, "If we're going to die, let's go out with a bang. Did you get my double entendre?"

"Yeah," Wakabayashi said.

"Get it?"

"Yeah."

"Get it?"

"Yeah."

"Get it?"

"Yeah. Double entendre." Wakabayashi said.

At about ten that night, Marlboro and Wakabayashi woke up hungry. Marlboro said, "Can I get you something to eat?"

"Sure."

"What would you like?"

"What are you having?" She asked.

"I'm going to make myself a liverwurst with mayo and onion on toasted Wonder bread."

"Mmm, that sounds good."

"And to drink?"

"What are you drinking?"

"Coca-Cola."

"Hmm, I'll have milk."

"Two liver cheese on a board, one moo juice, and one Atlanta coming right up," Marlboro said as he strolled into the kitchen naked.

When he returned with the goods, he found Wakabayashi had gotten dressed.

"Hey, what's with all the threads?" Marlboro asked.

"Johnny, I don't like to get crumbs all over my bits."

"Mmm, I would have Hoovered them up."

"As delightful as that sounds, I think we might be expecting some uninvited guests soon, and I wouldn't want you to be caught with your pants down when they arrive, if you know what I mean, and I think you do."

"I got ya, doll," Marlboro said as he slipped on his tattered old Levi 501 jeans, worn-out Harley Davidson tee shirt, and a bulletproof vest. After they had eaten, he helped her into her bulletproof vest, set her in the living room facing the apartment windows hidden behind a wall of sandbags with two Browning A5 12-gauge shotguns, an Ithaca Model 1911 A1 .45 pistol, and a Browning Automatic Rifle BAR all with hundreds of rounds of ammunition. He left her wearing a WWII US Army M1 Helmet with a built-in walkie-talkie and six MK3 concussion grenades.

"Listen, doll, if things look like they're going tits up, get into the bookcase and stay there until I get to you, understand?"

"Roger that. Where are you going to be?"

"I'll be roaming from the basement to the roof and all points in between. We've got a lot of booby traps to slow things down to where we will be controlling the action. Now remember, when they start to come in through the window, blow the bolts on the fire escape. Got it?"

"Yeah, I got it."

"Once they're inside, be sure to slip on your night vision goggles. Because when that F-104 Starfighter's landing lights start flashing on and off. I guarantee you that they'll be so discombobulated that they'll be stepping blindingly into the trays of electrified water under the windows that I rigged in the living room and bedroom, or if they make it past those, they'll get snared in one of the dozens of the "mantraps" scattered on the living room floor. Once they're inside the apartment, do not hesitate to open fire. Remember, they're here to kill you, so shoot first and ask questions later," He said and gave her a deep, passionate kiss.

BUZZZZZZ BUZZZZZZ

"That's the signal that someone is breaking into the basement. This is it, doll, be cool. You'll do fine. Keep talking to me on the walkie-talkie. Gotta run."

"Johnny."

"Yeah?"

"Love you," Wakabayashi whispered.

"Love ya too, doll."

Marlboro grabbed his Thompson submachine gun and eight drum magazines. He stuffed a 9mm Parabellum Browning machine pistol and a Semi-automatic Colt M1911 .45 caliber into his belt, and off he ran down the stairs to the basement to greet his unannounced visitors.

Chapter Twenty-Four
Subterranean Homesick Blues

Shugo Chiya and Isao Kombu, being the two thinnest of Little Tokyo's Black Rain gang, were assigned the task of entering the paint store through the basement window. Having learned from Atsuki Ryujin's gruesome experience, Shugo Chiya and Isao Kombu thought they had prepared themselves by wearing steel-soled workmen's boots; the thought was that they would avoid injury if they stepped on the metal spikes that caused Ryujin to lose his foot.

They stood utterly still once they had entered the basement, trying to get their bearings. The cellar was pitch black, as Marlboro had removed all the lightbulbs. Shugo Chiya and Isao Kombu brought flashlights with them that they shined all around the basement, looking for any booby traps. They saw none. They slowly made their way to the staircase leading to the main floor.

Shugo Chiya, being the oldest, ordered Kombu to take the lead. Kombu reluctantly eased his way up the stairs; his left foot broke through the pine tread when he got five steps up. The steel-soled shoe did protect him from the razor-sharp metal spikes. However, they didn't save him from the downward-angled spikes Marlboro installed that caught Isao Kombu's ankle and lower leg when he tried to pull his foot out. The harder he tried to remove his foot, the more the spikes dug in and began to shred and catch his leg.

Isao Kombu screamed out in agony.

EEEEYAAAARRGH!

Shugo Chiya tried to help by pulling on Kombu's leg. But the more he pulled, the more damage he did to Kombu. Finally, Isao passed out from the sheer pain, which caused Chiya to decide to retreat. Unfortunately for him, the window they had entered was too high to exit from, and there wasn't anything in the basement to help him.

He figured his only option was to either sit tight and hope that someone would pass by the alley and assist him in escaping, which would brand him a coward, or he could take his chances and try to go up the stairs. He chose the latter. Chiya got a running start and took the stairs two at a time, hoping to avoid any rigged steps.

Seeing that Isao got caught on stair number five, he assumed the booby-trapped steps were all uneven five, seven, nine, and eleven. He was wrong. He felt pretty confident, taking steps two, four, six, and eight until he hit step ten.

CRASH

The pain was the worst he had ever experienced. It was a white, blinding, excruciating shooting pain. He had almost made it; he was so close; only two more steps, and he would have been home free. He was teetering on the brink of unconsciousness when he heard the door at the top of the stairs open. Standing in the doorway was a figure of a man, backlit, holding what looked to him as a Tommy Gun. Chiya instinctively reached for his gun. The last thing he remembered seeing was the barrel flash of the "the Chicago typewriter" just before his and Isao Kombu's bodies were riddled with dozens of .45 caliber bullets, leaving their remains looking like nothing but a big gooey pile of succotash.

RATATATTRATTATATATRATTRATT

Chapter Twenty-Five
Knockin' On Heaven's Door

Wakabayashi was hunkered down behind the pile of sandbags when she heard the gunshots from the basement.

"Marlboro, are you okay?"

"I'm Jake. Stay sharp, doll; it's all beginning to unfold. I'm headed up to the main floor. Talk soon."

She thought she heard voices outside in the alley and footsteps on the fire escape. After a cursory check of her weapons, she eased the safety off the Browning Automatic Rifle and set it atop a sandbag facing the windows.

Kio Kobayashi and Hiroshi Takahashi parked down the street in the back seat of the black Lincoln Town Car, watching and waiting for the assault to officially begin. They had heard gunfire coming from the basement; apparently, Shugo Chiya and Isao Kombu didn't wait for Hagihara and the main attack to begin at midnight.

"I fear we've already lost Chiya and Kombu," Kobayashi said.

"What time is it?" Takahashi asked.

Kobayashi looked at his Rolex Submariner, "It's exactly midnight."

Just then, two tow trucks roared down from opposite ends of 1st Street. They came to a screeching halt in front of *Natsukashī Kokoro* (the Nostalgic Heart) paint store. Two men jumped out of each truck and attached two large hooks with chains to the shop's front door handle. They attached the chains to the back of their trucks and waited.

Seconds late, three Ford sedans filled with men carrying guns came spilling out of the cars and stood by eagerly waiting for the tow trucks to rip the door off its hinges. They didn't have to wait long. Yuuma Hagihara stood between the two trucks and raised his hand to signal the drivers to ready themselves. The drivers revved their 425 horse-powered v8 engines to their redlines, and once Hagihara dropped his hand, they both dropped the clutch; their tires screeched and smoked, and the door of the paint store flew off like a cat on a hot tin roof.

"*Banzai*!" Hagihara screamed as he pulled his *katana* from its sheath, held it over his head, and led the charge of fifteen howling, screeching, and yowling fanatics rushing into the blackness of the paint store, shooting and firing their weapons helter-skelter. They began knocking over displays and shooting cans of paint until Hagihara stood on the landing that led up to the apartment and shouted, "Let's spread out, find and kill the *gaijin*.

It was then that the overhead sprinkler system with a mixture of black oil base paint and a poly-acrylic adhesive went off, raining down on the rabid horde and covering them with a blinding sticky thick oil sludge that covered them entirely. The floor became as slippery as an ice rink; the more they tried to run, the more they would slip and fall, causing them to become covered with the gunk even more. As hard as they tried, they couldn't wipe it off, and it would only make things worse. It was then that Marlboro instigated the ultimate humiliation; he turned on the overhead ceiling fans and released two hundred pounds of chicken feathers that flew down, swirling around like a blizzard in Anchorage.

It was then, when the chaos was at its peak, that Marlboro stepped out from the shadows; he calmly aimed his

Thompson submachine gun and screamed as he fired, "Eat lead, motherfuckers!"

RATATATTRATTATATATRATTRATT RATATATTT RATTATATATRATTRATT RATATATTRATTATATAT

Hagihara stood alone, looking like Al Jolson wearing a Liberace decorative feathered boa. When he saw Marlboro, he raised his *katana* and started to charge his archenemy. Unfortunately, the floor was so slippery that he ran in place, screaming obscenities. Marlboro reached behind and pulled the Ithaca Model 1911 A1 .45 pistol that was tucked in his belt, aimed, and fired one shot, striking Hagihara in the forehead.

Marlboro tucked the revolver back into his belt and said, "That's what you get for bringing a sword to a gunfight."

When the smoke had cleared and the feathers settled, fifteen of Kobayashi and Takahashi's top yakuza lay dead in a sea of sludge, and feathers mixed with blood and an assortment of colored paints.

Marlboro scanned the field of death, making sure that he hadn't missed anyone before rushing upstairs to cover the roof. The silence was deafening as he stood looking over the slaughter and carnage. He could barely make out the paint and feathered covered bodies through the gun smoke. Once satisfied that they were all dead, he booked it up the stairs; he stopped by to see if Wakabayashi was okay.

"Johnny, are you all right? I heard all the screaming and gunfire, and I got so frightened," Wakabayashi cried.

"Not to worry, doll. It's all going to plan. You got to keep it together. They'll be trying the fire escape and the roof next. It's almost over. I'll come back down if you need me; just radio me. Love ya," Marlboro said as he dashed up the stairs to the roof.

Kobayashi and Takahashi, still sitting in the back seat of the black Lincoln Town Car, watched with excitement as the hordes rushed into the paint store, screaming and firing their guns. From where they were sitting, all they could see were the muzzle flashes and the thunderous roar of chaotic gunfire until there was silence, then a pillowy cloud of white chicken feathers wafting out the front door.

Kobayashi and Takahashi looked at each other in disbelief at what they saw; at first, they thought that Hagihara had succeeded in killing Baker, but as the feathers came billowing out onto the street, they began to fear the worst.

"Kyo, go see what is going on," Kobayashi ordered.

"*Hai, oyabun.*" The driver replied as he ran down the street and cautiously approached the *Natsukashī Kokoro* door. He stood there peeking in as he was showered with chicken feathers. Minutes later, he came running back.

"Well?" Kobayashi asked.

"They're all dead, *oyabun.*"

"Where was Hagihara?" Takahashi asked.

"He was dead, too. They are all covered in black oil and feathers. No one was moving. They're all dead, *oyabun*," Kyo said.

Trying to put a positive spin on the situation, Kobayashi said, "We still have an assault on the roof and from the alley. Kyo, take us around to the alley."

"*Hai, oyabun.*"

When they pulled into the alley, they could observe eight men climbing up the fire escape and half a dozen men repelling down the windows of the Mikado Hotel onto the roof of the *Natsukashī Kokoro* paint store.

"It won't be long now," Kobayashi boasted.

Chapter Twenty-Six
She Came In Through The Bathroom Window

Officer Hana Wakabayashi had been one of the highest-ranking marksmen in her class at the police academy, but that was on the shooting range. She had never fired her weapon in anger during a siege before. The time was fast approaching when she would be tested to her capacity. She could feel the adrenaline starting to course through her veins. She was both scared and totally invigorated.

The sounds of men's voices and footsteps clanging up the fire escape were getting closer. She lowered her night vision goggles, cocked the lever on the Browning Automatic Rifle, curled her index finger around the trigger, took a deep breath, and waited. She didn't have to wait long before she heard the scratching of a glass cutter, first on the bathroom window and then in the living room.

All the lights in the apartment had been shut off at the fuse box. She could see figures peering into the room using flashlights with the aid of her night vision goggles. The first man entered through the bathroom window. He wasn't paying attention to where he was stepping and planted both feet into a tray of electrified water, causing instant electrocution; he cried out. He collapsed on the floor, and a yellow plume of smoke rose from his head.

YEEEAHHHH!

The odor of burnt flesh filled the room as two figures came bursting into the living room off of the fire escape. Once they were inside the living room, a blast of retina-searing light flared up for less than two seconds, just long enough to make them disorientated, inducing temporary blindness and causing them to stumble, arms outreached, trying to feel their way, resulting in their stepping onto the mantraps. Where large steel springs snap shut, bringing sharp teeth crushing and breaking their leg above the ankle. The more the victim struggled, the more the claws dug deeper into the flesh. Their screams were so painful to hear that Hana could stand it no longer and took pity on them and fired several rounds, putting the poor souls out of their misery.

RATATATTRAT RATATATRATT RATATATTT

After two more men attempted to enter through the apartment windows, Hana pulled the lever, releasing the bolts holding the fire escape and forcing the entire structure to collapse with the three men waiting for their chance to enter the apartment fell to their deaths after the whole weight of the framework toppled down upon them crushing the life out of them.

The two men inside the living room stood motionless, their hands in the air, as if they were about to surrender. But as Hana stood up, the men grabbed for their weapons, a fatal mistake; her instincts kicked in, and she fired a burst of gunfire, sending both men flying backward and out the windows that they had minutes before climbed through.

RATATATTRAT RATATATRATT RATATATTRAT RATATATRATT RATATATTT

Kobayashi and Takahashi sat with their mouths agape as the fire escape collapsed, and two men flew out the window after being shot.

Takahashi had seen enough, "Take me back to the hotel."

"Kyo, let's go," Kobayashi said. To the driver.

"No. Kobayashi, you stay here and watch the end of this disaster. You'll be hearing from me!"

Kobayashi got out of the Lincoln and watched it drive away. His only chance of redemption would be if the men on the roof could possibly succeed where the others couldn't.

He positioned himself in the alley to get a better view of the attack. He could recognize the men's faces; none were wearing face coverings. The leader of the assault was Makoto Shinazugawa, the longtime gangster of the Black Rain and a cruel enforcer. He had served Kobayashi as a loyal arm-twister and bone-breaker for over two decades. With his hand still in a cast, he had jimmy-rigged it to hold his Colt – Police .38 Special by taping it with plenty of duct tape.

The others were equally as dedicated to the yakuza; just about all of them have the mark of the *Yubitsume* (cutting off a portion of one's left little finger above the top knuckle) and full-body tattoos.

Sogo Hakashita and Touki Gouma, two of Kobayashi's top drug dealers, spotted Kobayashi in the alley, held up their clenched fists, and shouted down to him, "*Banzai!*"

Kobayashi returned the salute and yelled, "*Banzai!*"

Chapter Twenty-Seven
Up On The Roof

Marlboro got to the roof minutes before Makoto Shinazugawa and the others began to repel down from the Mikado Hotel windows onto the *Natsukashī Kokoro's* roof; he hid behind the air conditioner's condenser unit.

He sat there and waited with his Tommy Gun cocked and ready. He spotted Makoto Shinazugawa struggling to repel down the rope with his hand in a cast, but giving credit where credit is due, Marlboro was genuinely impressed at Shinazugawa's sheer determination. The others had a much easier time abseiling from the hotel windows.

Once down, the men gathered around Shinazugawa for their orders. From a distance, it looked as if several men had brought Molotov cocktails, figuring that they would set the place on fire. When he saw that, Marlboro decided to target those men first. The group of eight formed a straight line, separated by three for four feet between them. Shinazugawa held up his hand with the cast and shouted, "*Banzai!*"

They began to run at full speed toward Marlboro. The men holding the Molotov cocktails lit the rag wick and were about to throw them when they reached the spring-loaded nail and screw boards. The four-inch nails penetrated the soles of their boots, causing them to instinctively drop their Molotov cocktails, breaking and engulfing them in flames. The other attackers, including Shinazugawa, continued on, but eventually, each of them became entangled in one of the booby traps. Once they were all caught in a trap, Marlboro rose from behind the air conditioner and opened fire.

RATATATTRAT   RATATATRATT   RATATATTRAT RATATATRATRATATATTRATT RATATATTRATRATRAT

The fire from the Molotov cocktails eventually burned itself, thanks in large part to the fire-resistant paint that Marlboro had laid down for such an eventuality.

Down in the alley, Kobayashi watched as his last ditched effort literally went up in flames. Dejected, he walked home just as a dozen police cars and fire trucks arrived, along with every TV station camera crew and newspaper reporter, and began to hover around like a swarm of bees.

Detective Tanaka, dozens of uniformed officers, as well as the medical examiner were astounded at what they discovered when they entered the paint store—bodies covered in what looked to be crude oil and covered with feathers. In the apartment, they found Officer Wakabayashi sitting on a pile of sandbags with a Browning Automatic Rifle across her lap, several bodies with their legs caught in what resembled bear traps, and one man found in the bathroom who appeared to have been electrocuted.

Tanaka met Marlboro on the roof, leaning against the air conditioner, Tommy Gun tucked under his arm, and seemingly staring off into space.

"Marlboro. Looks like you and Wakabayashi had a busy night." Tanaka said as he was about to wander out into the middle of the roof. To where the Black Rain's men lay dead

"I wouldn't do that, Detective."

"How come?"

Marlboro picked up a loose board and tossed it out onto the roof setting off several of the booby traps, four-inch nail traps, to spring up.

"Is that what happened to those men?" Tanaka asked, gesturing to the eight bodies lying twenty yards away.

Marlboro just nodded.

"How many?" Tanaka asked.

"I lost count. I don't know how many Wakabayashi bagged. From what I could tell, there was a lot inside the apartment, and I'm not sure about the ones killed when the fire escape collapsed."

"Looks like shooting fish in a barrel," Tanaka quipped.

"It was never meant to be a fair fight. There aren't any Marquess of Queensberry rules in a street fight. You know that, Yuki. So, I don't want any politician to start crying about morality and the evils of vigilante justice. The city wanted us to eliminate the Black Rain, which we did.

"From what I can tell, you two pretty much wiped out Little Tokyo's chapter of Black Rain."

"Well, at least for now."

Chapter Twenty-Eight
Epilogue

Kio Kobayashi was ordered back to Tokyo the week following the massacre at the *Natsukashī Kokoro* paint store. He was met at the airport by two of *Saikōshidō-sha* Hiroshi Takahashi's torpedoes, Tōro Busujima and Yuta Doumekii.

They wore the typical yakuza uniform: Ray-Ban sunglasses, sharkskin suits, cowboy boots with silver tips, and black shirts with skinny ties.

When Kobayashi stepped off the plane and was met by Takahashi's goons, neither of them talked to him. As they walked through the airport terminal, he had one of them walk on either side of him. When they got outside, a black Mercedes was waiting for them. Nothing was spoken during the ride from the airport to the Marunouchi district. Marunouchi is between the Imperial Palace and Tokyo Station, one of Japan's most prestigious business districts. It is home to the headquarters of many of Japan's most influential companies, particularly those in the financial sector. The offices of the Black Rain sit on Nakadori Avenue, tucked in between Mr. Yakatori Café and a Nikon Camera Store.

Things hadn't changed a lot since the last time Kobayashi was there. Although the last time he was there, it was under totally different circumstances. He had been handpicked to run the Little Tokyo chapter of the Black Rain. His future was bright; he was the fair-haired boy going to America to make his mark, and now things looked bleak. He was returning in shame. Under his tutelage, he lost close to forty men, either killed or arrested. In recent months, the Black Rain had posted losses of well over a million dollars in revenue. All because of the *gaijin* paint store owner Butch Baker and his whore. Kobayashi feared the worst; he only hoped that his act of contrition might save him.

When he entered the Saikōshidō-sha's (the supreme leader's) office, he bowed and stood at attention, waiting for permission to speak. Takahashi sat behind a large American oak desk. He was smoking a Cuban cigar and had a bottle of I.W. Harper bourbon and two glasses on his desk.

"Sit down, Kobayashi-san," Hiroshi Takahashi said.

Kobayashi did as he was told. He sat directly across from the *oyabun*. Takahashi picked up the bottle of whiskey, poured two glasses full, and shoved a glass over to Kobayashi.

"Drink up," He said as he took a sip of whiskey.

Kobayashi grabbed the glass and emptied the glass in one gulp. Now that he had steeled himself with some whiskey, he placed a small wooden box on the desk and slowly slid it toward Takahashi.

"Takahashi-san, I beg your forgiveness for my failure. I hope you will accept this as a sign of my loyalty."

Takahashi opened the box and saw the little finger from Kobayashi's left hand from performing *Yubitsume*.

"Kobayashi-san, if only this were enough. But I fear not. Because the catastrophe under your leadership can only be settled by the *Bushidō* Code," Takahashi said.

"Is there nothing that I can do to avoid *seppuku*?"

"The alternative is far worse. I fought for an honorable death, Kobayashi-san. The board wanted a more gruesome and violent punishment."

"When?"

"Tomorrow. Noon. But tonight, you will be a guest at my *fūzoku* host club. There, you will be plied with food, wine, drugs, and, of course, *sekkusu* (sex). We have the most beautiful *gaijins* from all over the world. Go and enjoy," Takahashi said.

After a night of total debauchery in which Kobayashi ate over fifteen hundred dollars of sushi, drank a three hundred dollar bottle of wine, consumed four thousand dollars' worth of cocaine, and had sex with three young blond women from Finland. When Takahashi came to collect him, Kobayashi was three sheets to the wind.

"I trust you had a pleasant evening, Kobayashi-san?"

"*Hai, arigatō* (yes, thank you)."

"It is time to go."

Takahashi and Kobayashi sat in the back of the black Mercedes and were driven to Itabashi City. They parked in front of a small private residence surrounded by a twelve-foot-tall fence on *Wakagi Dori* Street.

In the backyard, six top Black Rain Yakuza International members sat emotionlessly, as if they were about to watch a rerun of I Love Lucy. As *Saikōshidō-sha,* Takahashi took his place in the center, with three men seated on either side.

Placed in front of them the traditional mat where Kobayashi would kneel and the *sanbo* (a small wooden stand where the *tantō* would be placed), Kobayashi was allowed to bathe in cold water to prevent excessive bleeding. He dressed in a white kimono and was served sake. As he drank the sake, he hoped that he would die with as much dignity as Aoi Yamaguchi had done several months ago.

After he had finished, the *tantō* and cloth were handed to Kobayashi as he knelt on the mat. Standing directly behind him was a master swordsman, Shun Onigahara, acting as the *kaishakunin* (care worker) appointed to behead Kobayashi.

Kobayashi opened his kimono, picked up the *tanto*, held the blade with the cloth around it, and plunged the blade into his abdomen, making a left-to-right cut. Shun Onigahara, the *kaishakunin,* quickly and skillfully performed a *dakikubi* (embraced head) in which a slight band of flesh is left, attaching the head to the body so that the head can dangle in front as if embraced.

Once the *seppuku* was over, all the present leaders of the Black Rain went inside for lunch while two low-level lackeys rolled Kobayashi's body up in a rug and drove him out to the *Itabashi-ku* garbage dump.

Over lunch, Takahashi recommended that the Black Rain take some time before rushing back into Little Tokyo. For the time being, he suggested they build up the organization in San Francisco before returning to the City of Angels. He felt that there was more to the destruction of the LA Chapter than just a *gaijin* paint store owner and his whore.

"We shall bide our time. Our day shall come," Takahashi said.

However, he would never see that day come because three years later, he was shot in the head as a result of a bloody coup by his Number Two.

Takahashi forgot the golden rule of crime. Keep your friends close, but your enemies closer.

"Good morning, Los Angeles; this is Katie O'Connell. I'm in Little Tokyo at the scene of what can only be described as a bloodbath here at Natsukashī Kokoro, the Nostalgic Heart Paint Store located at 333 1ˢᵗ Street, next door to the landmark Mikado Hotel, where my sources tell me that a gun battle raged on for more than twenty minutes before the police and fire departments responded.

It appears that the incident all began when members of the notorious Japanese mafia gang known as the Black Rain attempted to break into the paint store but were met with heavy resistance by store owner Butch Baker and his Japanese wife.

According to police, Mr. Baker had anticipated such an attack and set up multiple booby traps as well as being heavily armed. Eyewitnesses claim to have seen the Black Rain try to enter the paint store from many different points of entry, climbing in through the basement window, crashing through the front door, climbing up the fire escape, and repelling down from the Mikado Hotel windows down onto the roof with Molotov Cocktails.

It would seem that Mr. Baker met each assault with superior force. Mr. Backer and his wife, Aiko Sugimoto Baker, have refused any attempt for an interview, as has Detective Sergeant Yuki Tanaka, who is leading the investigation. His only comment was that the police are looking into the incident and will release a full report on their investigation when the time is right.

At last count, the medical examiner, Doctor Gyening, told this reporter that he had counted twenty-eight dead, no wounded. Known Black Rain boss Kio Kobayashi was not available for comment. It has been rumored that Mr.

Kobayashi has left Los Angeles for Japan. However, we cannot confirm or disconfirm this information.

Here is what we do know about Butch Baker. He was a pilot during the war. He flew B-25s in the Pacific. After the war, he was stationed in Yokohama for three years, where he met Aiko after her parents were killed in the bombing of Hiroshima.

They met in a sushi bar where she worked as a waitress. They dated for the last two years of his service in Japan and were married in Tokyo in a civil service.

Butch is originally from Van Nuys; after the war, they decided to live in Little Tokyo to give Aiko a sense of community since leaving her homeland and culture.

Back to you, Chuck. This is Katie O'Connell for KTLA News."

Since the gunfight at *Natsukashī Kokoro*, the Nostalgic Heart Paint Store, the city council, the mayor's office, and the LAPD haven't breathed a word of the incident. No investigative reports have been issued, nor will there ever be one. Whenever inquiries were made, the parties being asked stalled until things settled down. Since then, the mayor has been re-elected, as have all the city council members on a strict law and order ticket. As for Detective Sergeant Yuki Tanaka, he has been promoted to Lieutenant and reassigned to the Ramparts Division.

Officer Hana Wakabayashi was promoted to the rank of Police Officer III and was assigned to the Police Academy as an Instructor.

"Good morning, Los Angeles; this is Katie O'Connell. It's been over a year since the massacre at Natsukashī Kokoro, the Nostalgic Heart Paint Store located at 333 1ˢᵗ Street, next door to the landmark Mikado Hotel, where over thirty members of the notorious Japanese mafia gang known as the Black Rain were killed by store owners Butch and Aiko Baker. Since then, the store has long since closed, and the Bakers have moved away. Numerous rumors have floated around. One is that they have moved up to Portland, Oregon, north of Cannon Beach, and have opened a candle shop; another is that they are in Nevada outside of Area 51 and run a roadside diner called The Alien Café. The most absurd rumor is that they booked passage on a tramp steamer and are now operating a PEZ candy store in Maputo, the capital of Mozambique.

I sense that they're somewhere in Southern California and just waiting for the heat to be off before resurfacing. I have a personal message for Butch and Aiko Baker, we are on your side, and although there are no known photographs of you, we will find you.

Also, we at KTLA have received hundreds of letters in support of you and thousands of dollars that people donated to you. We have opened a bank account in your name, so whenever you contact us, we will happily arrange for the money to be transferred to an account of your choice. A grateful Los Angeles thanks you. Now, back to you, Chuck. This is Katie O'Connell for KTLA News."

An anonymous caller identifying himself as Butch Baker contacted KTLA and had the collected money in the amount of eight thousand dollars sent to the "Save the Children" fund of Los Angeles.

Marlboro's fire-engine red 1946 Chevrolet Fleetmaster Convertible, with its 216.5 cubic inch, 3.5-liter engine screaming down Pacific Coast Highway, top down, was listening to *Sh-Boom* by The Crew-Cuts on KFWB. He had one hand on the suicide knob attached to the steering wheel and the other wrapped around Officer Hana Wakabayashi's shoulder.

When they reached the Sunset Boulevard exit, he made a wicked left turn and headed up the Pacific Palisades toward downtown L.A. Marlboro was adept at managing the twisting right and left chicanes that cut through Brentwood, under the 405 Freeway, into Westwood and Hollywood.

"Johnny, I'm getting hungry," Wakabayashi said.

"Hang on, doll. We're almost there."

"Oh, Johnny, not The Original Pantry Café!"

"Yeah, baby. I'm in the mood for some real 'merican food."

He parked the Fleetmaster out front in a towaway zone, threw the keys to the valet, and said, "Keep an eye on it, kid. There's a fiver in it for you."

"Yes, sir, Mr. Marlboro."

When Betty saw Marlboro walk in, she cried out, "Hey, Johnny boy. How the Hell are you? It's been ages!"

"Hey, doll. Oh, how I've missed ya."

"Come on in. I've got your table ready for you," she said as she led Marlboro and Wakabayashi to a dimly lit table in the corner, just like he liked it.

"Say, Betty, you remember Miss Wakabayashi?"

"Sure. How ya doing, honey?"

"I'm good, and how have you been?"

"Never better. Now, what can I get you kids to drink?"

Wakabayashi said, "I think I'll just have some water."

"One city juice, and for you?"

"I'll have my usual, a Bull Dog Stout."

"You got it. I'll get those and be right back to take your order."

Marlboro turned to Wakabayashi, held her hand, and said, "Isn't this nice?"

"Swell."

"Come on. I know this isn't as elegant as some *kaiseki* (an expensive restaurant), but it's good food."

Betty returned with the drinks and asked, "What'll it be?"

Wakabayashi said, "I'll have the pork chop with mashed potatoes and a salad with tomatoes."

Betty shouted out, "Gimme a flat car in a fog with cow feed with love apples."

Marlboro smiled and ordered, "I'll take a steak, rare, and an order of French fries."

"I need a slab of moo; let him chew it and one order of frog sticks."

"Thanks, doll," Marlboro said as Betty scampered off.

Wakabayashi gazed over a Marlboro, smiled, and said, "A slab of moo?"

Before Kobayashi left for Tokyo, he hired his own private dick, a Japanese American named Bintēji Foster, who also did private contract killing, to find and kill Butch Baker and his wife.

It took him a couple of months, but he discovered that Butch Baker was really John Marlboro, an ex-cop turned private investigator, and his so-called wife was actually police officer Hana Wakabayashi. And although he had gotten word that Kobayashi had met with an unfortunate end, he had been paid in advance; Foster's policy was that he always completed the job once paid, no matter what.

After dinner at the café, Marlboro and Wakabayashi headed back to her apartment on Venice Beach. Marlboro, who normally can spot a tail in seconds, was so preoccupied with Wakabayashi sitting next to him that he didn't notice the blue Ford Falcon with the two shady-looking occupants.

The ride down Santa Monica Boulevard was uneventful until they turned left onto Lincoln Boulevard, where a minor fender bender had occurred. It was then that Marlboro became aware of the blue Ford Falcon. He could either try to see if he could lose them or continue to Wakabayashi's apartment and let it play out. Marlboro never wanted to let things drag out.

"Listen, doll, we've picked up a tail somewhere. I'm thinking we should go to your place and duke it out."

"Do you think that's wise?" She asked.

"They probably know where you live already, and we can end this now and be done with it."

"You have a gat?" She asked.

"Always," He said, grinning.

Marlboro parked the fire-engine red Fleetmaster in front of her apartment on Milwood Court. He walked around to open her door and escort her into the building. As he did, he casually got a glance at the two goons in the blue Ford.

Wakabayashi's apartment was on the third floor, next to the elevator. Once they got inside, she locked and bolted the door. She entered the bedroom, got her service revolver, and double-checked to ensure it was loaded.

"How do you want to handle this?" Wakabayashi asked.

"Well, they'll most likely wait until we turn off the lights and go to bed. They're probably on the street now, watching. Once they think we're asleep, they'll pick the locks and come in to kill us."

"You don't think they just want to talk to us?"

"If they wanted to talk, they would have been up here knocking on your door."

They waited with the lights on for half an hour, setting up the bed to look like they were in bed. They used pillows to resemble their bodies, and she put a wig sticking out from under the covers, which in the dark looked rather convincing. They hid under the bed with guns drawn.

From out in the living room, they heard the fate sounds of locks being picked and the soft patter of footsteps. Marlboro whispered to Wakabayashi, "Get ready. Aim for their legs."

They could see the bedroom door silently open and the silhouette of two men's legs. As they approached the bed, Marlboro and Wakabayashi aimed at their legs, and Marlboro whispered, "Fire."

BLAM! BLAM! BLAM! BLAM! BLAM! BLAM!

Bintēji Foster dropped onto the floor; he was facing Marlboro. Marlboro stuck his Ithaca Model 1911 A1 .45 pistol in Foster's face and pulled the trigger two more times.

BLAM! BLAM!

Spattering half of Mr. Bintēji Foster's face and brains all over Officer Hana Wakabayashi's bedroom walls as his partner, Roger Peterman, was writhing in pain on the floor. Wakabayashi scrambled out from under the bed, pointing her service revolver at the man as she kicked his gun away from him.

Marlboro rolled out from under the bed and turned on the overhead lights. He picked Peterman up and plopped him in the rocking chair on the corner.

"Okay, who the Hell are you guys, and why were you trying to kill us?" Marlboro asked.

"I need a doctor!" Petermen shouted.

Marlboro sapped the thug on the side of his head with his roscoe and said, "If you don't start talking, I'll blow your brains out like your friend over there. Ya dig?"

"But I'm bleeding."

Marlboro pulled the trigger back and said in a cool, calculating tone, "I'm going to count to three. And if I'm not hearing names, I'll blast ya. One…Two…"

"I'm Roger Peterman, and he's Bintēji Foster."

"Why were you going kill us?"

"I need to go to a hospital."

"If you don't start talking, you'll be going to the morgue. Now stop whining and start talking!"

"Bintēji Foster's a private dick. He was hired to whack you and the broad."

"Who hired him?"

"I don't know, some Jap big shot."

"Name?"

"I don't know."

Marlboro placed the barrel of his Ithaca .45 on Peterman's head and said, "One…Two…"

"I don't know his real name; it's Japanese, something like Kobe, Kobayakawa?"

"Kobayashi?" Marlboro asked.

"Yeah. That's it, Kobayashi."

"But he's dead," Wakabayashi said.

Marlboro leaned into Peterman's face and asked, "When did Kobayashi hire Foster?"

"I don't know, maybe three months ago. It was before he headed off to Japan."

"And did he tell you why he put the hit on us?"

"No. Foster didn't tell me, and honestly, I didn't want to know. Now, can I get to a hospital?"

"Sure. Once the cops get here, Wakabayashi, call Lieutenant Tanaka."

While waiting for the Calvary to arrive, Marlboro bandaged Peterman's legs.

"You'll live. Police Officer Wakabayashi didn't hit any arteries." Marlboro said.

It took twenty minutes before Tanaka and a couple black and whites to arrive. Tanaka looked at the mutilated face of Bintēji Foster and asked, "Marlboro, who or what is that?"

"That is, Bintēji Foster, PI and hitman. That one sitting in the rocker and bleeding all over Wakabayashi's rug is Roger Peterman, Foster's assistant."

"Why did they want to put the whack on you and Wakabayashi?"

"It seems that Kobayashi hired Foster to find and kill the Bakers before he left for Tokyo. Do you know this mutt?" Marlboro asked.

"Yeah, I know him. Bintēji Foster was a small-time goon who did a stretch in San Quentin for armed robbery. We pinched him a couple of times for assault and battery, and extorsion. But he always seemed to beat the rap by intimidating witnesses."

"Well, he's not so intimidating now," Marlboro quipped.

"You know, Marlboro, you're a one-man wrecking crew. Everywhere you go, death and destruction seems to follow," Tanaka said.

"What can I tell you, Lieutenant? I don't start fights. I finish them."

After the medical examiner, the EMT fellas carted off Roger Peterman, Lieutenant Tanaka, and the boys in blue left Marlboro, and Wakabayashi stood in the bedroom looking at the bloody mess.

"Well, I know some cleaners at the department I can call on to come in here and clean up this mess," Wakabayashi said.

"You can't stay here; let's go to my place. I got a nice bottle of sake that we can crack open."

"Sake?"

"Yeah, you know, I think I'm turning Japanese; I really think so," Marlboro smirked.

Owari

The End

JAPANESE GLOSSARY

Aisupikku: Ice pick
Arigatō: Thank you
Asagutsu: low wooden clogs

Baishunpu: Whore
Baka: Fool
Banzai: Hurrah
Beddo ni kite: Come to bed
Bokushi: Reverend
Bushidō Code: The way of the warrior
Buta: Pig

Chabudai: A short-legged table
Chan: An honorific for close friends or lovers
Chōzuya: Cleansing fountain

Dakikubi: Embraced head
Damare: Shut up
Dōitashimashite: Your welcome
Dōke: Buffoon
Dono: Master

Emboshi: a tall purple hat worn by Shintō priests

Fakkumī: Fuck me
Fakkuyū: Fuck you
Fundoshi: Loincloth

Gaichū; Vermin
Gaijin: Foreigner
Gesu yarō: Asshole
Gorira: Gorilla

Hahaoya baka: Mother fucker
Hai: Yes
Hai, arigatō: Yes, thank you
Haiden: Hall of worship
Hara-kiri: Belly cutting
Heitai: Soldiers
Hiwacha: Finch-brown

Īe: No
Iku ka shinu ka: Go or die
Irezumi: Full-body

Jōsō: the everyday garb of Shintō priests
Jishin: Earthquake

Kaiseki: An expensive restaurant
Kaishakunin: the person appointed to behead the
                one performing *seppuku.*
Kame: Turtle
Kami: Gods
Kamishimo: Top and bottom

Kamikaze: Japanese pilots assigned to make a suicidal crash on a target

Kanpai: Cheers

Kanri: Top-level management

Kare no migite: His right hand

Kariyasu: Japanese triandra grass

Kashikomarimashita: Yes sir

Kasuri: Pattern woven cotton fabric cloth

Kensei: Sword saint

Kin'yōbi wa daijōbudeshou: Friday will be fine

Kokoro: Heart

Kon'nichiwa: Hello

Komainu: Lion-like creatures meant to ward off evil spirits

Kōnaiseikō: Oral sex

Konbanwa: Good evening

Koroshi-ya: Hitmen

Korosu: Kill

Kōshaku e: To the Duke

Koshinukes: Cowards

Kōtei banzai: Long live the Emperor

Kōun o: Good luck

Kuroi Ame: Black Rain

Kuso: Fuck

Kuso ttare: God damnit

Kuso yarō: Asshole

Kutabare: Fuck it

Kyaputen: Captain

Masutā: Master

Meinu: Bitch

Misutādōnatsu: Mister Donut

Moshi moshi: Hello

Nanite Kokoda: Oh my God
Natsukashī: Nostalgic
Naze: Why

Ochoko Small ceramic cup
Ohayō: Good morning
Ohayōgozaimasu: Good morning
Oi: Hey
Oicho-Kabu: Japanese card game
Orokamono: Idiots
Oyabun: Boss
Owabi moushi agemasu: I apologize

Panku: Punk

Rōjin: Old man
Rokudenashi: Bastard
Rokōcha: Contemplation in a tea garden
Rōnin: A samurai for hire
Rosanzerusu e yōkoso: Welcome to Los Angeles

Sāikō: Let's go
Saikōshidō-sha: The supreme leader
Saké: Japanese rice wine
Sanbo: A small wooden stand
Sandō: Worshipper's path
Sayōnara: Goodbye
Sensei: Teacher
Senshi: Warriors
Seppuku: Cutting the belly

Shaku: A baton carried by Shintō priests
Shazai itashimasu: Deepest apology
Shikkō-sha: Enforcers
Shimada mage: Traditional formal hairstyle for unmarried women
Shinta ka Hitoshi-jima: Dead island
Shinjimae: Go to Hell
Shinshoku: Shintō priest
Shinu toki ga kita yo, rōjin: Time to die, old man
Shiori Koibito: White lover
Shirako: Fish prostate
Shuriken: Throwing stars
Sore ga jinseida: Such is life
Sore o shimatte kudasai: Put that away
Sore wa okonawa rerudearou: It shall be done
Soto de mate: Wait outside

Tadaaki: Faithful light
Tamago-iro: Egg-colored
Tatami: A type of flooring mat
Tantō: A short sword
Tawagoto: Shit
Tawagoto no ichibu: Piece of shit
Tokkuri: Saké bottle
Torisashi: Raw chicken
Tsuma: Wife

Wakatta: Okay

Watashi no saiai: My dearest

Yakuza: Japanese organized crime syndicate

Yamabukicha: Gold-brown
Yoi: Good
Yoi tomodachi: Good friend
*Yoiichinichiwo***:** Have a nice day
Yoru no sutōkā: The night stalker
Yubitsume: the cutting off a portion of one's left
little finger above the top knuckle

1950s GLOSSARY

APB: All Points Bulletin
A side of Joan of Arc: An order of French Fries
Axle grease: butter

Babe: Woman
Bangtails: Racehorses
Behind the eight-ball: In a difficult position
Bent as a butcher's hook: Someone who is gay
Berries and Cherries: Police car lights
Big house: Prison
Big sleep: Death
Big-wigs: The rich & powerful
Bloodhound in the hay: Hotdog with sauerkraut
Blow: Leave
Blow one down: Kill someone
Blowing smoke: Lying
Boof: Anal sex
Bop: To kill
Bossy in a bowl: Beef stew
Breeze off: Get lost
Broderick: A thorough beating
Bruno: Tough guy, enforcer
BTO: Big Time Operators
Bump: Kill; also, **bump-off**: a killing
Bupkis: Nothing
Business: Work over; beating
Button man: Professional killer

Capo: A leader of a "crew"
Cement shoes: A method of body disposal
Cheaters: Sunglasses
Cheese it: Hide
Chicago lightning: Gunfire
Chicago overcoat: Coffin
Chicago typewriter: Thompson machine gun
Chin music: Punch on the jaw
Chinese angle: A strange twist
Chinese Molasses: Opium
Chink: Chinese
Chippie: Woman of easy virtue
Chopper squad: Men with machine guns
Church key: Various kinds of bottle openers
Clams: Dollars
Clipped: Shot
Clubhouse: Police station
Coffin nails: Cigarettes
Coldcock: To knock someone down
Contract: A favor
Copper: Policeman

Deep pockets: People with a lot of money
Dewars flask: A vacuum flask, i.e., thermos
Dick: Private investigator
Dingus: A thing or item
Double sawbuck: $20 bill
Drift: Go, leave
Drill: Shoot
Drink out of the same bottle: Close friends
Drop a dime: To inform on someone

Duck soup: Easy, a piece of cake

Enforcer: Debt collector for a loan shark

Fish-wrappers: Newspapers
Five-spot: $5 bill
Fry: To be electrocuted

Gams: Legs (especially a woman's)
Gat: Gun
Geezer: An old person
Get under your skin: To annoy
Glad rags: Fancy clothes
Glitterati: People who love the cameras
Goombah: Member of a criminal gang
Greasers: A hoodlum, thief, or punk
Grift: Swindle
Gripe my cookies: Irritate or disgust
Gum-shoe: Detective
Gunsel: Gunman

Hack: Newspaper reporter
Hash house: A cheap restaurant
Hatchet men: Killers, gunmen
Heat: A gun
Heater: A gun
High pillow: Person at the top, in charge
Hinky: Suspicious
Hitting the pipe: Smoking opium
Hit the bricks: Leave
Hold your breath for it: Taking the rap
Honcho: Leader

Hockey Puck: Hamburger, well done
Hooch: Whiskey
Hood: Criminal
Hot seat: Under great pressure

Jackrabbit parole: To escape from jail
Jake: Okay
Jam: Trouble, as in "in a jam"
Jamoke: A dimwit
Jobbie: Man
Joe: Coffee, as in "a cup of joe"

Kerfuffle: A commotion or fuss
Kibosh: To stop
Knock off: Kill
Knuckle sandwich: Punch in the mouth

Large: $1,000; **twenty large:** $20,000
Lead poisoning: To be shot
Loogan: A guy with a gun
Looker: Pretty woman

Made Man: A mobster that has killed someone
Make it Cry: Add onion to a Hamburger
Manyak: Bastard
Meat wagon: Coroner's vehicle
Mishegoss: Craziness, lunacy
Moniker: Name
Motor: A police officer who rides a motorcycle
Mouthpiece: Lawyer
Moxie: Guts, nerve
Muckety-muck: a person of great importance

Muff it: Make a mistake
Mug: Face
Mugs: Men (esp. dumb ones)
Murphy: Potato

Oat soda: Beer
On the hoof: Rare Hamburger

PCH: Pacific Coast Highway
PDQ: Pretty Damn Quick
Palooka: Bum
Peeper: Detective
Plug ya: Shoot someone
Pop: Kill
Popped: Killed
Pulchritudinous: Beautiful
Pumped full of lead: Multiple gun wounds
Put the lights out and cry: Liver and onions

QT: In confidence or secretly

Rod: Gun
Roscoe: Gun
Rub-out: A killing
Rube: A bumpkin
Rumble: The news

Sap: A blackjack
Sap: A dumb guy
Sapping: Getting hit with a sap
Sawbuck: $10 bill
Scratch: Money

Scuttlebutt: Gossip
Sfortunato: An unlucky guy
Shamus: Private Detective
Shanked: Stabbed
Shiv: Homemade knife
Skate around: To be of easy virtue
Snooper: Detective
Spick and span: Spotlessly clean
Square: Honest
Stitch up: Put someone in danger
Stir: Prison
Stronzo: Asshole

Take it on the lam: To try and escape
Take the fall for: Accept punishment for
Tea: Marijuana
Three-spot: Three-year term in jail
Throw away gun: An unregistered gun to be used once and thrown away
Throw lead: Shoot bullets
Ticket: P.I. license
Tip their mitt: Reveal something
Tomato: Pretty woman
Tooting the wrong ringer: Asking the wrong person
Torpedoes: Gunmen
Trigger man: A man whose job is to use a gun
Trouble boys: Gangsters
Twist: A confident, strong woman

Weak sister: A push-over
Whack: Kill

Wheel: An influential person
Wooden kimono: A coffin

Yap: Mouth

M. Ward Leon – the Author

M. Ward Leon is a former advertising creative director who began his career at Doyle Dane Bernbach in New York during the Mad Men era. While at DDB, his writing for the Volkswagen Rabbit campaign earned him inclusion in the Smithsonian Institution Advertising Archives. Recently, his writing garnered two Emmy Awards for Public Service advertising. He is a graduate of California State University, Los Angeles, and an alumnus of Art Center College of Design.

Other books by M. Ward Leon: *Blood of the Beast* • *Revenge of the Beast* • *Wounding of the Beast* • *The Strange and Curious Cases of Roscoe Brown, Detective NYPD* • *Ambush at Fig Tree Gulch* • *Ishmael. My Life After Moby Dick* • *City of Angeles Trilogy* • *The Fine Art of Murder*